Stories from the T

Stories from the Trenches

by Carleton B. Case

Copyright © 2/9/2016
Jefferson Publication

ISBN-13: 978-1523969623

Printed in the United States of America

All rights reserved. No part of this book may be reprinted or reproduced or utilized in any form or by any electronic, mechanical, or other means, now known or hereafter invented, including photocopying and recording, or in any form of storage or retrieval system, without prior permission in writing from the publisher.'

Table of Contents

THE MAN WHO "CAME BACK" 4
    FOUR TO THE GOOD 8
FRANCO-YANKO ROMANCES 8
    CUTE, WASN'T SHE? 12
    EVERY ONE TO HIS TASTE 13
TRENCH SUPERSTITIONS 13
IN THE TRAIL OF THE HUN 15
    SOME STUNT—TRY IT 19
    WHEN THE HUN QUIT SMOKING 20
WHEN "ACE" LUFBERY BAGGED NO. 13 20
    HORSE AND HORSE 22
    WHY TOMMY JOINED THE CHURCH 22
LIFE AT THE FRONT 22
THE "FIDDLER'S TRUCE" AT ARRAS 26
HARRY LAUDER DOES HIS BIT 27
    CAUSE FOR GRIEVANCE 29
    DOUBLY ANNOYING 29
KING GEORGE UNDER FIRE 29
    THE FEMALE STANDARD OF SIZE 31
STORY OF OUR FIRST SHOT 31
    HE KNEW WHAT TO DO 32
    THAT WAS THE HYMN NUMBER 32
STORIES FROM THE FRONT 33
    FUNNY THEY HADN'T MET 34
    NO END TO THE GAME 34
UNCLE SAM, DETECTIVE 34
    DRIVING IS TOO GOOD FOR THEM 40
    NOW THEY DON'T SPEAK 41
DIDN'T RAISE HIS BOY TO BE A "SLACKER" 41
    CONSOLING INFORMATION 42
    HE WAS ALL RIGHT 42
THE 100-POUND TERROR OF THE AIR 43
THE WATCH-DOGS OF THE TRENCHES 45
    ALL IN THE SAME COUNTRY 47
GENERAL BELL REDEEMS HIS PROMISE 48
    NO GREAT LOSS 49
LETTERS FROM THE FRONT 49
    HELPING HIS WIFE OUT 53

MEET TOMMY, D. C. MEDAL MAN	53
GERMAN FALCON KILLED IN AIR-DUEL	55
HE TAUGHT THE "TANK" TO PROWL AND SLAY	57
NOT A SELF-STARTER	59
TRY IT ON YOUR WIFE	59
HE WAS GOING AWAY FROM THERE	59
TAKING MOVING PICTURES UNDER SHELL-FIRE	59
COSTS MORE NOW	63
WEIGHTY MEASURES INVOLVING UNCLE SAM'S NAVY	63
NEVER TALK BACK	65
GOING HOME	65
ENLISTED MEN TELL WHY THEY JOINED THE ARMY	65
THE NATIONAL GAME	67
TOMMY ATKINS, RAIN-SOAKED AND WAR-WORN STILL GRINS	67
SOMETHING NEW FOR THE MARINES	69
JUDGING BY HIS LETTERS	71
BLESS THESE AMATEURS	71
NEW GROUNDS FOR EXEMPTION	71
SOUSA'S LITTLE JOKE	72
RAPID MILITARY ADVANCEMENT	72

THE MAN WHO "CAME BACK"

ONE of the strangest of the many personal romances which the war has brought is the tale of a man who, dismissed from the British Army by court martial, redeemed himself through service with that most heterogeneous of organizations, the French Foreign Legion. His name was John F. Elkington, and he had held an honored post for more than thirty years. Then, just as his regiment, in the closing months of 1914, was going into the fighting on the Western front, he was cashiered for an unrevealed error and deprived of the opportunity to serve his country.

Heavy with disgrace, he disappeared, and for a long time no one knew what had become of him. Some even went so far as to surmise that he had committed suicide, until finally he turned up as an enlisted soldier in the Foreign Legion. In their ranks he went into the conflict to redeem himself. Today, says the New York *Herald*, he is back in England. He will never fight again, for he has practically lost the use of his knees from wounds. But he is perhaps the happiest man in England, and the account tells why, explaining:

Pinned on his breast are two of the coveted honors of France—the Military Medal and the Military Cross—but most valued possession of all is a bit of paper which obliterates the errors of the past—a proclamation from the official London *Gazette* announcing that the King has "graciously approved the reinstatement of John Ford Elkington in the rank of lieutenant-colonel, with his previous seniority, in consequence of his gallant conduct while serving in the ranks of the Foreign Legion of the French Army."

Not only has Colonel Elkington been restored to the Army, but he has been reappointed in his old regiment, the Royal Warwickshires, in which his father served before him.

In the same London *Gazette*, at the end of October, 1914, had appeared the crushing announcement that Elkington had been cashiered by sentence of general court martial. What his error was did not appear at the time, and has not been alluded to in his returned hour of honor. It was a court martial at the front at a time when the first rush of war was engulfing Europe and little time could be wasted upon an incident of that sort. The charge, it is now stated, did not reflect in any way upon the officer's personal courage.

But with fallen fortunes he passed quietly out of the Army and enlisted in the Legion—that corps where thousands of brave but broken men have found a shelter, and now and then an opportunity to make themselves whole again.

Colonel Elkington did not pass unscathed through fire. His fighting days are ended. His knees are shattered and he walks heavily upon two sticks.

"They are just fragments from France," he said of those wounded knees, and smiled in happy reminiscence of all they meant.

"It is wonderful to feel," said Colonel Elkington, "that once again I have the confidence of my King and my country. I am afraid my career in the field is ended, but I must not complain."

Colonel Elkington made no attempt to cloak his name or his former Army service when he entered the ranks of the Legion.

"Why shouldn't I be a private?" he asked. "It is an honor for any man to serve in the ranks of that famous corps. Like many of the other boys, I had a debt to pay. Now it is paid."

The press of London is unanimous in welcoming the old soldier back into his former rank. One of them, *The Evening Standard*, contains the account of how he went about enlisting for France when he saw he would best leave London. It is written by a personal friend of Colonel Elkington, with all the vividness and sympathy of an actual observer of the incidents detailed. We are told:

"Late in October, 1914, I met him, his Army career apparently ruined. He had told the truth, which told against him; but in the moment when many men would have sunk, broken and despairing, he bore himself as he was and as he is today, a very gallant gentleman. He had been cashiered and dismissed from the service for conduct which, in the judgment of the court martial, rendered him unfit and incapable of serving his sovereign in the future in any military capacity. The London *Gazette* came out on October 14, 1914, recording the fact, and it became known to his many friends. For over thirty years he had served, and for distinguished service wore the Queen's medal with four clasps after the Boer War. He went to France with the Royal Warwickshire Regiment at the outbreak of this conflict. His chance had come after twenty-eight years."

During the first terrible two months he had done splendid work. A moment sufficient to try the discretion of any officer arrived. He made his mistake. He told his story to the general court martial. He vanished—home; and the London *Gazette* had the following War-Office announcement:

"Royal Warwickshire Regiment.—Lieutenant-Colonel John F. Elkington is cashiered by sentence of a general court martial. Dated September 14, 1914."

He recognized at once, as he sat with me, what this meant. We chatted about various projects, and at last he said, "There is still the Foreign Legion. What do you say?"

Being acquainted with it, I told him what I knew; how it was the "refuge" for men of broken reputations; how it contained Italians, Germans, Englishmen, Russians, and others who had broken or shattered careers; the way to set about joining it by going to the recruiting office at——; how the only requirement was physical fitness; that no questions would be asked; that I doubted if he would like all his comrades; that the discipline was very severe; that he might be sent to Algiers; that he would find all kinds of men in this flotsam—men of education and culture, perhaps scoundrels and blackguards as well; but he would soon discover perfect discipline.

Now for a man of his age to smile as he did, to set out on the bottom rung of the ladder as a ranker in a strange army, among strangers, leaving all behind him that he held dear, was a great act of moral courage. We heard of him at intervals, but such messages as dribbled through to his friends were laconic. We heard also he had been at this place and that, and that he was well and apparently doing well. That he had been repeatedly in serious action of recent months we also knew, and then came the news that he had won the coveted *Médaillé Militaire*—and more, that it was for gallant service. A curious distinction it is in some ways. Any meritorious service may win it; but not all ranks can get it. A *generalissimo* like General Joffre or Sir Douglas Haig may wear it for high strategy and tactics, and a non-commissioned officer or private may win and wear it for gallantry or other distinction. But no officer below a *generalissimo* can gain it. This distinction Elkington won. We all felt he had made good in the Legion, where death is near at all times, and we waited.

Today's *Gazette* announcement has given all who knew him the greatest pleasure. He has told none of them for what particular act he received the coveted medal—just like Jack Elkington's modesty.

But, as soon as he arrived home in England, the interviewers went after him hot and heavy. He found it all very boresome, for, now that the affair was over, he could see no use in talking about it to everybody. A reporter for *The Daily Chronicle*, however, managed to get what is probably the most satisfactory interview with him and one which shows to best advantage the peculiar psychology of this man who has experienced so many different sides of life. The interviewer, in telling of their conversation, portrays the Colonel as saying:

"Complaint? Good Lord, no! The whole thing was my own fault. I got what I deserved, and I had no kick against anyone. It was just 'Carry on!'"

Brave words from a brave man—a man who has proved his bravery and worth in what surely were as heartrending circumstances as ever any man had to face. My first sight of the Man Who Has Made Good was as he descended the stairs, painfully and with the aid of two sticks, into the hall of his lovely old home by the river at Pangbourne. It is a house which the great Warren Hastings once called home also.

Very genial, very content, I found the man whose name today is on everyone's lips; but very reticent also, with the reticence natural to the brave man who has achieved his aim and, having achieved it, does not wish it talked of.

"And now," I suggested, "you have again got what you deserve?"

Colonel Elkington drew a long breath. "I hope so," he said, at length, very quietly. "I have got my name back again, I hope cleared. That is what a man would care for most, isn't it?"

"There is always a place in the Foreign Legion for someone who is down in the world," he told me. "Directly after the court martial, when the result appeared in the papers, I said I must do something; that I could not sit at home doing nothing, and that as I could not serve England I would serve France. Yes, I did offer my services again to England, but it is military law that no man who has been cashiered can be employed again for the King while the sentence stands. So there was nothing for it but the Foreign Legion—that home for the fallen man."

Of that strange and famous corps Colonel Elkington cannot speak without a glint of pride in his keen blue eyes. Splendid men, the best in the world, he calls them, "and every one was as kind as possible to me." Many there were who had become legionaries because they, too, had failed elsewhere, "lost dogs like myself," the Colonel called them; but the majority of the men with whom he served were there because there was fighting to be done, because fighting was second nature to them, and because there was a cause to be fought for. The officers he describes as the "nicest fellows in the world and splendid leaders."

When Colonel Elkington first joined there were many Englishmen included in its ranks, but most of these subsequently transferred to British regiments. He enlisted in his own name, but none knew his story, and often he was questioned as to his reason for not transferring—"and I had to pitch them the tale."

He kept away from British soldiers as much as possible, "but one day someone shouted my name. I remember I was just about to wash in a stream when a staff motor drove by and an officer waved his hand and called out. But I pretended not to hear and turned away...

"I don't think that the men in the Legion fear anything," he said. "I never saw such men, and I think in the attack at Champaigne they were perfectly wonderful. I never saw such a cool lot in my life as when they went forward to face the German fire then. It was a great fight; they were all out for blood, and, though they were almost cut up there, they got the German trenches."

The time he was recognized, as detailed above, was the only one. At no other time did any of his comrades suspect his identity, or else, if they did, they were consideration itself in keeping it to themselves. Of this recognition and some of his subsequent experiences, the London *Times* remarks, speaking of its own interview with him:

It was the only voice from the past that came to him, and he took it as such. A few minutes afterward he was stepping it out heel and toe along the dusty road, a private in the Legion.

Shot in the leg, Colonel Elkington spent ten months in hospital and eight months on his back. This was in the Hôpital Civil at Grenoble. He could not say enough for the wonderful treatment that was given him there. They fought to save his life, and when they had won that fight, they started to save his leg from amputation. The head of the hospital was a Major Termier, a splendid surgeon, and he operated eight times and finally succeeded in saving the damaged limb. When he was first in hospital neither the patients nor any of the hospital staff knew what he was or what he had done. Elkington himself got an inkling of his good fortune at Christmas when he heard of his recommendation for the *Croix de Guerre*.

"Perhaps that helped me to get better," he said. "The medals are over there on the mantelpiece." I went over to where there were two glass cases hanging on the wall. "No, not those; those are my father's and my grandfather's." He showed me the medals, and on the ribbon of the cross there was the little bronze palm-branch which doubles the worth of the medal.

When he was wounded Dr. Wheeler gave him a stiff dose of laudanum, but he lay for thirteen hours until he saw a French patrol passing. He was then 100 yards short of the German second line of trenches, for this was in the Champaigne Battle, on September 28, when the French made a magnificent advance.

It was difficult to get Colonel Elkington to talk about himself. As his wife says, he has a horror of advertisement, and a photographer who ambushed him outside his own lodge-gates yesterday made him feel more nervous than when he was charging for the machine gun that wounded him. To say he was happy would be to write a platitude. He is the happiest man in England. He is now recuperating and receiving treatment, and he hopes that he will soon be able to walk more than the 100 yards that taxes his strength to the utmost at present.

FOUR TO THE GOOD

In times of peace Smith might have been an author who had drifted into some useful occupation, such as that of a blacksmith, but just now he is cook to the Blankshire officers' mess. Smith sent Murphy into the village to bring home some chickens ordered for the mess.

"Murphy," said Smith, the next day, "when you fetch me chickens again, see that they are fastened up properly. That lot you fetched yesterday all got loose, and though I scoured the village I only managed to secure ten of them."

"'Sh!" said Murphy. "I only brought six."

FRANCO-YANKO ROMANCES

THE story is told of a British "Tommy" who could not make up his mind whether to acquire a farm or a village store, by marriage, "somewhere in France." He could have either, but not both. Dispatches say that the banns have already been read for some of our "Sammies," and when the war is over France will have some sturdy Yankee citizens. Difference of language seems to form no bar; in fact, the kindly efforts of each to learn the language of the other acts as an aid. It must be said that the British, so far, have rather had the best of it. They have beaten the Yankees to the altar of Hymen, but they had the field to themselves for some time. By the end of the war the Americans may have caught up, for love and war have always walked hand in hand with Uncle Sam's boys. Nevertheless the British have a big start, for Judson C. Welliver, writing to the New York *Sun* from Paris, says that in Calais hundreds of young English mechanics have married French girls. The writer tells of being accosted by a young man from "the States" at the corner of the Avenue de l'Opéra and "one of those funny little crooked streets that run into it." Breezily the American introduced himself and said:

"Say, do you happen to know a little caffy right around here called the—the—blame it, I can't even remember what that sign looked like it was trying to spell."

I admitted that the description was a trifle too vague to fit into my geographic scheme of Paris.

"Because," he went on, "there's a girl there that talks United States, and she's been waiting on me lately. I get all the best of everything there and don't eat anywhere else. But this morning I took a walk and coming from a new direction I can't locate the place. I promised her I'd be in for breakfast this morning."

"Something nifty?" I ventured, being willing to encourage that line of conversation. Whereat he plainly bridled:

"She's a nice girl," he said; "family were real people before the war. Learned to talk United States in England; went to school there awhile. Why, she wouldn't let me walk home with her last night, but said maybe she would tonight."

There isn't anybody quite so adaptable as the young Frenchwoman. Only in the last few months has Paris seen any considerable number of English-speaking soldiers, because earlier in the war the British military authorities kept their men pretty religiously away from the alleged "temptations" of the gay capital. Later they discovered that Paris was rather a better place than London for the men to go.

So the French girls, in shops and cafés, have been learning English recently at an astounding rate. They began the study because of the English invasion; they have continued it with increased zeal because since the Americans have been coming it has been profitable.

To be able to say "Atta boy!" in prompt and sympathetic response to "Ham and eggs" is worth 50 centimes at the lowest. The capacity to manage a little casual conversation and give a direction on the street is certain to draw a franc.

Besides, there aren't going to be so many men left, after the war, in France!

Mademoiselle, figuring that there are a couple of million Britishers in the country and a million or maybe two of Americans coming, has her own views about the prospect that the next generation Frenchwomen may be old maids.

In Calais there is a big industrial establishment to which the British military authorities have brought great numbers of skilled mechanics to make repairs to machinery, reconstruct the outworn war-gear, tinker obstreperous motor-vehicles, and, in short, keep the whole machinery and construction side of the war going. Most of the mechanics who were sent there were young men.

Calais testifies to the ability of the Frenchwomen to make the most of their attractions. English officers tell me that hundreds of young Englishmen settled in Calais "for the duration" have married French girls and settled into homes. They intend, in a large proportion of cases, to remain there, too.

The same thing is going on in Boulogne, which is to all intents and purposes nowadays as much an English as a French port. Everywhere English is spoken and by nobody is it learned so quickly as by the young women.

Frenchwomen have always had the reputation of making themselves agreeable to visiting men, but one is quite astonished to learn the number of Englishmen who married Frenchwomen even before the war. The balance is a little imperfect, for the records show that there are not nearly as many Frenchmen marrying English girls. But, says the writer in the *Sun*, a new generation of girls of marriageable age has arrived with the war, and:

Not only in the military, industrial, and naval base towns are the British marrying these Frenchwomen, but even in the country nearer the front. There are incipient romances afoot behind every mile of the trench-line.

Two related changes in French life are coming with the war which make these international marriages easier. Both relate to the *dot* system. On the one side there are many French girls who have lost their *dots* and have small prospect of reacquiring the marriage portion. To live in these strenuous times is about all they can hope for. For these the free-handed Americans, Canadians, and Australians look like good prospects for a well-to-do marriage.

Even the British Tommy, though he enjoys no such income as the Americans and colonials, is nevertheless quite likely to have a bit of private income from the folks "back in Blighty" to supplement the meager pay he draws. The portionless French maid sees in these prosperous young men who have come to fight for her country not only the saviors of the nation, but a possibility of emancipation from the *dot* system that has broken down in these times.

On the other side, there are more than a few young women in France who must be rated "good catches" to-day, though their *dots* would have been unimportant before the war. A girl who has inherited the little property of her family, because father and brothers all lie beneath the white crosses along the Marne, not infrequently finds herself possessed of a little fortune she could never have expected under other conditions. Many of these, likewise, bereft of sweethearts as well as relatives, have been married to English and colonial soldiers or workmen; and pretty soon we will be learning that their partiality for America—for there is such a partiality, and it is a decided one—will be responsible for many alliances in that direction.

How it will all work out in the end is only to be guessed at as yet. The British officers who have been observing these Anglo-French romances for a long time assert that the British Tommy who weds a Frenchwoman is quite likely to settle in France; particularly if his bride brings him a village house or a few hectares of land in the country.

On the other hand, the colonials insist on taking their French brides back to New Zealand or Canada, or wherever it may be—India, Shanghai, somewhere in Africa—no matter, the colonial is a colonial forever; he has no idea of going back to the cramped conditions of England. He likes the motherland, all right, is willing to fight for it, but wants room to swing a bull by the tail, and that isn't to be had in England, he assures you.

Probably the Americans will be like the colonials; those who find French wives will take them home after the war. That a good many of them will marry French wives can hardly be doubted.

Yes, the French girls like the American boys. But there is another scene. It is that of the country billet, which varies from a château to a cellar, the ideal one—from the point of view of a billeting officer—being a bed for every officer, and nice clean straw for the men. Get this picture of "Our Village, Somewhere in France," back of the line, as drawn by Sterling Hielig in the Los Angeles *Times:*

A French valley full of empty villages, close to the fighting line. No city of tents. No mass of shack constructions. The village streets are empty. Geese and ducks waddle to the pond in Main Street.

It is 4 o'clock a. m.

Bugle!

Up and down the valley, in the empty villages, there is a moving-picture transformation. The streets are alive with American soldiers—tumbling out of village dwelling-houses!

Every house is full of boarders. Every village family has given, joyfully, one, two, three of its best rooms for the cot beds of the Americans! Barns and wagon-houses are transformed to dormitories. They are learning French. They are adopted by the family. Sammy's in the kitchen with the mother and the daughter.

Bugle!

They are piling down the main street to their own American breakfast—cooked in the open, eaten in the open, this fine weather.

In front of houses are canvas reservoirs of filtered drinking-water. The duck pond in Main street is being lined with cement. The streets are swept every morning. There are flowers. The village was always picturesque. Now it is beautiful.

Chaplains' clubs are set up in empty houses. The only large tent is that of the Y. M. C. A.; and it is *camouflaged* against enemy observers by being painted in streaked gray-green-brown, to melt into the colors of the hill against which it is backed up, practically invisible. Its "canteen on wheels" is loaded with towels, soap, razors, chocolate, crackers, games, newspapers, novels, and tobacco. At cross-roads, little flat Y. M. C. A. tents (painted grass and earth color) serve as stations for swift autos carrying packages and comforts. In them are found coffee, tea, and chocolate, ink, pens, letter-paper, and envelopes; and a big sign reminds Sammy that "You Promised Your Mother a Letter, Write It Today!"

All decent and in order. Otherwise the men could never have gone through the strenuous coaching for the front so quickly and well.

In "Our Village," not a duck or goose or chicken has failed to respond to the roll call in the past forty days—which is more than can be said of a French company billet, or many a British.

Fruit hung red and yellow in the orchards till the gathering. I don't say the families had as many bushels as a "good year"; but there is no criticism.

In a word, Sammy has good manners. He looks on these French people with a sort of awed compassion. "They had a lot to stand!" he whispers. And the villagers, who are no fools ("as wily as a villager," runs the French proverb), quite appreciate these fine shades. And the house dog wags his tail at the sight of khaki, as the boys come loafing in the cool of the back yard after midday dinner.

In the evening the family play cards in the kitchen, and here no effort is necessary to induce the girls to learn English, for, though they pretend that they are teaching French, they are really—very slyly—"picking up" English while they are being introduced to the mysteries of draw-poker. Says the writer in *The Times:*

So, it goes like this when they play poker in the kitchen—the old French father, the pretty daughter, the flapper girl cousin, and three roughnecks. (One boy has the sheets of "Conversational French in Twenty Days," and really thinks that he is conversing— "*Madame, mademoiselle, maman, monsieur, papa,* or *mon oncle,* pass the buck and get busy!")

"You will haf' carts, how man-ny? (business.) Tree carts, fife carts, ou-one cart, no cart, an' zee dee-laire seex carts!"—"Here, Bill, wake up!"—"Beel sleep! *Avez-vous sommeil,* Beel?"—"*Oui,* mademoiselle, I slept rotten last night, I mean I was *tray jenny pars'ke* that darned engine was pumping up the duck pond—"

"Speak French!"—"Play cards!"—"*Vingt-cinq!*"—"*Et dix!*" "*Et encore five cen-times.* I'm broke. Just slip me a quarter, Wilfred, to buy *jet-toms!*" And a sweet and plaintive voice: "I haf' tree paire, *mon oncle,* an' he say skee-doo, I am stung-ed. I haf' seex carts!"—"Yes, you're out of it, I'm sorry, mademoiselle. Come up!" "Kom opp? Comment, kom opp?"

"Stung-ed" has become French. Thus does Sammy enrich the language of Voltaire. His influence works equally on pronunciation. There is a tiny French village named Hinges— on which hinges the following. From the days of Jeanne d'Arc, the natives have pronounced it "Anjs," in one syllable, with the sound of "a" as in "ham"; but Sammy, naturally, pronounces it "hinges," as it is spelled, one hinge, two hinges on the door or window. So, the natives, deeming that such godlings can't be wrong on any detail, go about, now, showing off their knowledge to the ignorant, and saying, with a point of affection: "I have been to 'Injes!'"

I should not wonder if some of these boys would marry. They might do worse. The old man owns 218 acres and nobody knows what Converted French Fives. Sammy, too, has money. A single regiment of American marines has subscribed for $60,000 worth of French war-bonds since their arrival in the zone—this, in spite of their depositing most of their money with the United States Government.

Sammy sits in the group around the front door in the twilight. Up and down the main street are a hundred such mixed groups. Already he has found a place, a family. He is somebody.

And what American lad ever sat in such a group at such a time without a desire to sing? And little difference does it make whether the song be sentimental or rag; sing he must, and sing he does. The old-timers like "I Was Seeing Nellie Home" and "Down by the Old Mill Stream" proved to be the favorites of the listening French girls. For they will listen by the hour to the soldiers' choruses. They do not sing much themselves, for too many of their young men are dead. But, finally, when the real war-songs arrived, they would join timidly in the chorus, "Hep, hep, hep!" and "Slopping Through Belgium" electrified the natives, and *The Times* says:

To hear a pretty French girl singing "Epp, epp, epp!" is about the limit.

Singing is fostered by the high command. Who can estimate the influence of "Tipperary?" To me, American civilian in Paris, its mere melody will always stir those noble sentiments we felt as the first wounded English came to the American Ambulance Hospital of Neuilly. For many a year to come "Tipperary" will make British eyes wet, when, in the witching hour of twilight, it evokes the khaki figures in the glare of the sky-line and the dead who are unforgotten!

Who can estimate, for France, the influence of that terrible song of Verdun—"*Passeront pas!*" Or who can forget the goose-step march to death of the Prussian Guard at Ypres, intoning "*Deutschland Uber Alles!*"

"It is desired that the American Army be a singing army!" So ran the first words of a communication to the American public of Paris, asking for three thousand copies of "The Battle Hymn of the Republic"—noble marching strophes of Julia Ward Howe, which 18641865 fired the hearts of the Northern armies in 1864-1865.

Mine eyes have seen the glory of the coming of the Lord! . . .

They are heard now on the American front in France. One regiment has adopted it "as our marching song, in memory of the American martyrs of Liberty." And in Our Village, you may hear a noble French translation of it, torn off by inspired French grandmothers!

I have seen Him in the watch-fires of a hundred circling camps;

They have builded Him an altar in the evening dews and damps;

I have read His righteous sentence by the dim and flaring lamps;

His day is marching on.

Bear with me to hear three lines of this notable translation. Again they are by a woman, Charlotte Holmes Crawford, of whom I had never previously heard mention. They are word for word, vibrating!

Je L'ai entrevu Qui planait sur le cercle large des camps,

On a érigé Son autel par les tristes et mornes champs,

J'ai relu Son juste jugement à la flamme des feux flambants,

Son jour, Son jour s'approche!

It's rather serious, you say? Rather solemn?

Sammy doesn't think so.

CUTE, WASN'T SHE?

He was a young subaltern. One evening the pretty nurse had just finished making him comfortable for the night, and before going off duty asked: "Is there anything I can do for you before I leave?"

Dear little Two Stars replied: "Well, yes! I should like very much to be kissed good-night."

Nurse rustled to the door. "Just wait till I call the orderly," she said. "He does all the rough work here."

EVERY ONE TO HIS TASTE

Visitor—"It's a terrible war, this, young man—a terrible war."

Mike (badly wounded)—"'Tis that, sor—a tirrible warr. But 'tis better than no warr at all."

TRENCH SUPERSTITIONS

IT is told in the chronicles of "The White Company" how the veteran English archer, Samkin Aylward, was discovered by his comrades one foggy morning sharpening his sword and preparing his arrows and armor for battle. He had dreamed of a red cow, he announced.

"You may laugh," said he, "but I only know that on the night before Crécy, before Poitiers, and before the great sea battle at Winchester, I dreamed of a red cow. To-night the dream came to me again, and I am putting a very keen edge on my sword."

Soldiers do not seem to have changed in the last five hundred years, for Tommy Atkins and his brother the *poilu* have warnings and superstitions fully as strange as Samkin's. Some of these superstitions are the little beliefs of peace given a new force by constant peril, such as the notion common to the soldier and the American drummer that it is unlucky to light three cigars with one match; other presentiments appear to have grown up since the war began. In a recent magazine two poems were published dealing with the most dramatic of these—the Comrade in White who appears after every severe battle to succor the wounded. Dozens have seen him, and would not take it kindly if you suggested they thought they saw him. They are sure of it. The idea of the "call"—the warning of impending death—is firmly believed along the outskirts of No Man's Land. Let us quote some illustrations from the Cincinnati *Times:*

"I could give you the names of half a dozen men of my own company who have had the call," said Daniel W. King, the young Harvard man, who was transferred from the Foreign Legion to a line regiment; just in time to go through the entire battle of Verdun. "I have never known it to fail. It always means death."

Two men were quartered in an old stable in shell-range of the front. As they went to their quarters one of them asked the other to select another place in which to sleep that night. It was bitterly cold and the stable had been riddled by previous fire, and the army blanket under such conditions seems as light as it seems heavy when its owner is on a route march.

"Why not roll up together?" said the other man. "That way we can both keep warm."

"No," said the first man. "I shall be killed to-night."

The man who had received the warning went into the upper part of the stable, the other pointing out in utter unbelief of the validity of a call that the lower part was the warmer, and that if his friend were killed it would make no difference whether his death chamber were warm or cold. A shell came through the roof at midnight. It was a "dud"—which is to say that it did not explode. The man who had been warned was killed by it. If it had exploded the other would probably have been killed likewise. As it was he was not harmed.

A few days ago the chief of an aeroplane section at the front felt a premonition of death. He was known to all the army for his utterly reckless daring. He liked to boast of the number of men who had been killed out of his section. He was always the first to get away on a bombing expedition and the last to return. He had received at least one decoration—accompanied by a reprimand—for flying over the German lines in order to bring down a *Fokker*.

"I have written my letters," he said to his lieutenant. "When you hear of my death, send them on."

The lieutenant laughed at him. That sector of the line was quiet, he pointed out. No German machine had been in the air for days. He might have been justified in his premonition, the lieutenant said, on any day of three months past. But now he was in not so much danger as he might be in Paris from the taxicabs. That day a general visited the headquarters and the chief went up in a new machine to demonstrate it. Something broke when he was three thousand feet high and the machine fell sidewise like a stone.

It is possible, say the soldiers, to keep bad fortune from following an omen by the use of the proper talisman. The rabbit's foot is unknown, but it is said that a gold coin has much the same effect—why, no one seems to know. A rabbit's foot, of course, must be from the left hind leg, otherwise it is good for nothing, and according to a *poilu* the efficacy of the gold piece depends upon whether or no it puts the man into touch with his "star." It is said in the New York *Sun:*

Gold coins are a mascot in the front lines, a superstition not difficult to explain. It was at first believed that wounded men on whom some gold was found would be better looked after by those who found them, and by degrees the belief grew up, especially among artillery, that a gold coin was a talisman against being mutilated if they were taken prisoners, whether wounded or not.

The Government's appeals to have gold sent to the Bank of France and not to let it fall into enemy hands in case of capture has since reduced the amount of gold at the front, but many keep some coins as a charm. Many men sew coins touching one another in such a way as to make a shield over the heart.

"Every man has his own particular star," a Lyons farm hand said to Apollinaire, "but he must know it. A gold coin is the only means to put you in communication with your star, so that its protecting virtue can be exercised. I have a piece of gold and so am easy in my mind I shall never be touched." As a matter of fact he was seriously wounded later.

Perhaps he lost his gold-piece!

The Sun relates another story which indicates the belief that if the man does not himself believe that he had a true "call" he will be saved. It is possible to fool the Unseen Powers, to pull wool over their eyes. To dream of an auto-bus has become a token of death, attested by the experience of at least four front-line regiments. And yet a sergeant succeeded in saving the life of a man who had dreamed of an auto-bus by the use of a clever ruse—or lie, if you prefer. As the anecdote is told in *The Sun:*

A corporal said he had dreamed of an auto-bus. "How can that be," the sergeant asked, "when you have never been to Paris or seen an auto-bus?" The corporal described the vision. "That an auto-bus!" declared the sergeant, although the description was perfect. "Why, that's one of those new machines that the English are using. Don't let that worry you!" He didn't, and lived!

A regiment from the south has the same belief about an automobile lorry.

But, unfortunately for the scientifically minded, a disbelief in omens does not preserve the skeptic from their consequences. On the contrary, he who flies in the face of Providence by being the third to get a light from one match is certain of speedy death. *The Sun* continues:

Apollinaire tells how he was invited to mess with a friend, Second Lieutenant François V——, how this superstition was discussed and laughed at by François V——, and how François V—— happened to be the third to light his cigaret with the same match.

The morning after, François V—— was killed five or six miles from the front lines by a German shell. It appears that the superstition is that the death is always of this nature, as Apollinaire quotes a captain of a mixed *tirailleur* and *zouave* regiment as saying:

"It is not so much the death that follows, as death no longer is a dread to anyone, but it has been noticed that it is always a useless form of death. A shell splinter in the trenches or, at best, in the rear, which has nothing heroic about it, if there is anything in this war which is not heroic."

IN THE TRAIL OF THE HUN

WAR has become so much a part of the life of the French peasants that they have little fear under fire. Frenchmen over military age and Frenchwomen pursue their ordinary avocations with little concern for exploding shells. To be sure, it is something of a nuisance, but children play while their mothers work at the tub washing soldier clothing. And as the Allied armies advance, wresting a mile or two of territory from the enemy at each stroke, the peasant follows with his plow less than a mile behind the lines. War has become a part of their lives. Newman Flower, of *Cassell's Magazine*, has been "Out There," and he thus records some of his impressions in the trail of the war:

The war under the earth is a most extraordinary thing. In the main, the army you see in the war zone is not a combatant army. It is the army of supply. The real fighters you seldom set eyes on unless you go and look for them. And, generally speaking, the ghastliness of war is carried on beneath the earth's level.

Given time, the *Boche* will take a lot of beating as an earth delver. At one spot on the Somme I went into a veritable underground town, where, till the British deluge overtook them, three thousand of the toughest Huns the Kaiser had put into his line lived and thrived. They had sets of compartments there, these men, with drawing-rooms complete, even to the piano, kitchen, bathroom, and electric light, and I was told that there was one place where you could have your photograph taken, or buy a pair of socks! Every visitor down the steps—except the British—was required to turn a handle three times, which pumped air into the lower regions. If you descended without pumping down your portion of fresh air you were guilty of bad manners.

Anything more secure has not been invented since Adam. But this impregnable city fell last year, as all things must fall before the steady pressing back of British infantry.

The writer tells of discovering in an old French town that was then under fire a shell-torn building on which were displayed two signs reading "First Aid Post" and "Barber Shop." He says:

When I dived inside I saw one man having his arm dressed, for he had been hit by a piece of shell in the square, and in a chair a few yards away a Tommy having a shave. Coming in as a stranger, I was informed that if I didn't want a haircut or a shave, or hadn't a healthy wound to dress, this was not the Empire music hall, so I had better "hop it."

It was in "hopping it" that I got astride an unseen fiber of British communication. I went into the adjoining ruins of a big building. A single solitary statue stood aloof in a devastation of tumbled brick and stone. Then, as I was stepping from one mound of rubble to another, as one steps from rock to rock on the seashore, I heard voices beneath me. The wreckage was so complete, so unspeakably complete, that human voices directly under my feet seemed at first startling and indefinite. Moreover, to add to my confusion, I heard the baa-ing of sheep, likewise under the earth. But I could see no hole, no outlet.

With the average curiosity of the Britisher I searched around till I discovered a small hole, a foot in diameter, maybe, and a Tommy's face framed in it laughing up at me.

"Hello!" he said.

I pulled up, bewildered, and looked at him.

"What in Heaven's name are you doing in there?" I asked.

"We're telephones.... Got any matches?"

"I heard sheep," I informed him.

"And what if you did? Got them matches?"

I tossed him a box. He dived into darkness, and I heard him rejoicing with his pals because he'd found some one who'd got a light. It meant almost as much to them as being relieved.

So here was a British unit hidden where the worst Hun shell could never find it, and, what was more, here was the food ready to kill when, during some awkward days, the *Boche* shells cut off supplies.

Then look on this picture of a war-desolated country where nature has been stupidly scarred by Teuton ruthlessness, and rubble-heaps are marked by boards bearing the name of the village that had stood there:

The desert was never more lonely than those vast tracts of land the armies have surged over, and this loneliness and silence are more acute because of the suggestions of life that have once been there. It is impressive, awe-inspiring, this silence, like that which follows storm.

Clear away to the horizon no hedge or tree appears, all landmarks have gone, hills have been planed level by the sheer blast of shells. Here is a rubble-heap no higher than one's shoulders where a church has stood, and the graves have opened beneath pits of fire to make new graves for the living. Patches of red powder, washed by many rains, with a few broken bricks among them, mark the places where houses, big and small, once rested. To these rubble-heaps, which were once villages, the inhabitants will come back one day, and they will scarcely know the north from the south. Indeed, if it were not for the fact that each rubble-heap bears a board whereon the name of the village is written, in order to preserve the site, they would never find their way there at all, for the earth they knew has become a strange country. Woods are mere patches of brown stumps knee-high—stumps which, with nature's life restricted, are trying to break into leaf again at odd spots on the trunks where leaves never grew before. Mametz Wood and Trone Wood appear from a short distance as mere scrabblings in the earth.

The ground which but a few months ago was blasted paste and pulverization has now under the suns of summer thrown up weed growth that is creeping over the earth as if to hide its hurt. Wild convolvulus trails cautiously across the remnants of riven trenches, and levers itself up the corners of sand bags. In this tangle the shell holes are so close that they merge into each other.

The loneliness of those Somme fields! No deserts of the world can show such unspeakable solitude.

One comes from the Somme to the freed villages as one might emerge from the desert to the first outposts of human life at a township on the desert's rim. Still there are no trees on the sky-line; they have all been cut down carefully and laid at a certain angle beside the stumps just as a platoon of soldiers might ground their arms. For the German frightfulness is a methodical affair, not aroused by the heat of battle, but coolly calculated and senseless. Of military importance it has none.

In these towns evacuated by the Germans life is slowly beginning to stir again and to pick up the threads of 1914. People who have lived there all through the deluge seem but partially aware as yet that they are free. And some others are returning hesitatingly.

Mr. Flower notes with interest the temperamental change that has been wrought by the war in the man from twenty to thirty-five years old. To the older ones it all is only a "beastly uncomfortable nuisance," and when it is over they will go back to their usual avocations. Here is the general view of the middle-aged men in the battle line:

"What are you going to do after the war?" I asked one.

I believe he thought I was joking, for he looked at me very curiously.

"Do?" he echoed. "I'm going to do what any sane man of my age would do. I'm going straight back to it—back to work. This is just marking time in one's life, like having to go to a wedding on one's busiest mail day. I'm not going to exploit the war as a means of getting a living, or emigrate, or do any fool thing like that. I'm going straight back to my office, I am. I know exactly where I turned down the page of my sales book when I came out—it was page seventy-nine—and I'm going to start again on page eighty."

With the younger men it is different. It has struck a new spark in them and fired a spirit of adventure. There are those who even enjoy the war, and to whom one day, when peace comes, life will seem very tame. The writer cites this case:

He is quite a young man, and what this adventurous fellow was before he took his commission and went to the war I do not pretend to know. But he displayed most conspicuous bravery and usefulness from the hour he fetched up at the British front.

One day he was very badly wounded in the back, and as soon as he neared convalescence he became restive and wished to return to his men, and he did return before he should have done. The doctor knew he would finish a deal quicker when he got back to the lines than he would in a hospital.

There are some rare creatures who are built that way. Shortly afterward he was wounded again, and while walking to the dressing station was wounded a third time, on this occasion very badly.

He stuck it at the hospital as long as he could—then one day he disappeared. No one saw him go. He had got out, borrowed a horse, and ridden back to his lines.

The absence of the fighting men from the view of an observer of a modern battle strongly impressed the writer, who says:

Most men who come upon a modern battle for the first time would confess to finding it not what they expected. For the old accepted idea of battle is hard to eliminate. One has become accustomed to looking for great arrays of fighters ready for the bout, with squadrons of cavalry waiting somewhere beyond a screen of trees, and guns—artfully hidden guns—bellying smoke from all points of the compass. The battle pictures in our galleries, the lead soldiers we played with as children and engaged in visible conflict, have kept up the illusion.

You know before you come to it that it is not so in this war, but this battle of hidden men pulls you up with a jolt as not being quite what you expected to see. You feel almost as if you had been robbed of something.

The first battle I saw on the western front I watched for two and a half hours, and during that time (with the exception of five men who debouched from a distant wood like five ants scuttling out of a nest of moss, to be promptly shot down) I did not see a man at all. The battle might have been going on in an enormous house and I standing on the roof trying to see it.

But if there is little or nothing to be seen of the human agents that direct the devastating machines of war during a battle, the scene of the field after the fight has been waged discloses all the horror that has not been visible to the eye of an observer. Mr. Flower thus describes one section of the theater of war in France:

Our car rushes down a long descending road, and is driven at breakneck speed by one of those drivers with which the front is strewn, who are so accustomed to danger that to dance on the edge of it all the time is the breath of life. To slow down to a rational thirty miles an hour is to them positive pain; to leap shell holes at fifty or plow across a newly made road of broken brick at the same velocity is their ecstasy. And one of the greatest miracles of the war is the cars that stand it without giving up the unequal contest by flying into half a hundred fragments.

But this road is tolerable even for a war road, and it runs parallel with a long down which has been scrabbled out here and there into patches of white by the hands of men. It is Notre Dame de Lorette, no higher than an average Sussex down, mark you, and lower than most. Yet I was told that on this patch of down over a hundred thousand men have died since the war began. Running at right angles at its foot is a lower hill, no higher than the foothill to a Derbyshire height, but known to the world now as Vimy Ridge. And this road leads you into a small section of France, a section of four square miles or so, every yard of which is literally soaked with the blood of men.

On the right is Souchez, and the wood of Souchez all bare stumps and brokenness; here the sugar refinery, which changed hands eight times, and is now no more than a couple of shot-riddled boilers, tilted at odd angles with some steel girders twirled like sprung wire rearing over them; and around this conglomeration a pile of brick powder. You wonder what there was here worth dying for, since a rat would fight shy of the place for want of a square inch of shelter. And where is Souchez River? you ask, for Souchez River is now as famous as the Amazon. Here it is, a sluggish sort of brook, crawling in and out of broken tree-trunks that have been blasted down athwart it, running past banks a foot high or so, a river you could almost step across, and which would be well-nigh too small to name in Devonshire.

We leave our cars under a bank and come on down through the dead jetsam of the village of Ablain St. Nazaire. The old church is still here on the left, the only remnant of a respectable rate-paying hamlet. The remaining portion of its square tower is clear and white, for the stonework has been literally skinned by flying fragments of steel, till it is about as clean as when it was built.

We reach the foot of Vimy Ridge and climb up. Here, some one told me, corn once grew, but now it is sodden chalk, pasted and mixed as if by some giant mixing machine with the shattered weapons of war.

Broken trenches—the German front line—in places remain and extend a few yards, only to disappear into the rubble where the tide swept over them.

As we climb, the earth beneath my foot suddenly gives way, letting me down with a jerk to the hip, and opening up a hole through which I peer and see a dead *Boche* coiled up, his face—or so I suspect it was—resting upon his arm to protect it from some oncoming horror.

We climb on up. We drop into pits and grope out of them again, pasted with the whiteness of chalk. From somewhere behind us a howitzer is throwing shells over our heads, shells that come on and pass with the rush of a train pitching itself recklessly out of control. We listen to the clamor as it goes on—a couple of miles or so—separating itself from the ill assortment of snarling and smashing and breaking and grunting that rises from the battlefield.

As they climbed the ridge the guns seemed to be muffled until they got beyond the shelter of Notre Dame de Lorette. Then, says the writer:

We suddenly appeared to tumble into a welter of sound. And the higher we climbed Vimy, the louder the tumult became. "Aunty," throwing over heavy stuff, had but a few moments before been the only near thing in the battle. Now the contrast was such as if we had been suddenly pushed into the middle of the battle. The air was full of strange, harsh noises and crackings and cries. And the earth before us was alive with subdued flame flashes and growing bushes of smoke.

Five miles away, Lens, its church spires adrift in eddies of smoke, appeared very unconscious of it all. Just showing on the horizon was Douai, and I wondered what forests of death lay waiting between those Lens churches and the Douai outlines where the ground was sunken and mysterious under the haze.

Here, then, was the panorama of battle. Never a man in sight, but the entire earth goaded by some vast invisible force. Clots of smoke of varying colors arrived from nowhere, died away, or were smudged out by other clots. A big black pall hung over Givenchy like the sounding-board over a cathedral pulpit. A little farther on the village of Angres seemed palisaded with points of flame. Away to the right the long, straight road from Lens to Arras showed clear and strong without a speck of life upon it.

No life anywhere, no human thing moving. And yet one believed that under a thin crust of earth the whole forces of Europe were struggling and throwing up sound.

Among all the combatants there is a desire for peace, says Mr. Flower, who found a striking example of the sentiment of the *Boche* in what had been the crypt of the Bapaume cathedral. He writes:

I saw scores of skulls of those who were dead many decades before the war rolled over Europe, and on the skull of one I saw scribbled in indelible pencil:

"*Dass der Friede kommen mag*"

("Hurry up, Peace.")—*Otto Trübner.*

Now, Otto Trübner may be a very average representative of his type. And maybe Otto Trübner's head now bears a passing likeness to the skull he scribbled on in vandal fashion before he evacuated Bapaume. But whether or no, he is, metaphorically speaking, a straw which shows the play of the wind.

SOME STUNT—TRY IT

Sergeant (drilling awkward squad)—"Company! Attention company, lift up your left leg and hold it straight out in front of you!"

One of the squad held up his right leg by mistake. This brought his right-hand companion's left leg and his own right leg close together. The officer, seeing this, exclaimed angrily:

"And who is that blooming galoot over there holding up both legs?"

WHEN THE HUN QUIT SMOKING

Tommy I—"That's a top-hole pipe, Jerry. Where d'ye get it?"

Tommy II—"One of them German Huns tried to take me prisoner an' I in'erited it from 'im."

WHEN "ACE" LUFBERY BAGGED NO. 13

LIEUT. GERVAIS RAOUL LUFBERY, an "Ace" of the Lafayette Escadrille, has brought down his thirteenth enemy airplane. The German machine was first seen by Lufbery—who was scouting—several hundred yards above him. By making a wide detour and climbing at a sharp angle he maneuvered into a position above the enemy plane at an altitude of five thousand yards and directly over the trenches. The German pilot was killed by Lufbery's first shot and the machine started to fall. The gunner in the German plane quickly returned the fire, even as he was falling to his death. One of his bullets punctured the radiator and lodged in the carburetor of Lufbery's plane, and he was forced to descend.

To a writer in the Philadelphia *Public Ledger* Lufbery describes the type of young man America will need for her air fleet. He says:

"It will take the cream of the American youth between the ages of eighteen and twenty-six to man America's thousands of airplanes, and the double cream of youth to qualify as chasers in the Republic's new aerial army.

"Intensive and scientific training must be given this cream of youth upon which America's welfare in the air must rest. Experience has shown that for best results the fighting aviator should not be over twenty-six years old or under eighteen. The youth under eighteen has shown himself to be bold, but he lacks judgment. Men over twenty-six are too cautious.

"The best air fighters, especially a man handling a 'chaser,' must be of perfect physique. He must have the coolest nerve and be of a temperament that longs for a fight. He must have a sense of absolute duty and fearlessness, the keenest sense of action and perfect sight to gain the absolute 'feel' of his machine.

"He must be entirely familiar with aerial acrobatics. The latter frequently means life or death.

"Fighting twenty-two thousand feet in the air produces a heavy strain on the heart. It is vital, therefore, that this organ show not the slightest evidence of weakness. Such weakness would decrease the aviator's fighting efficiency.

"The American boys who come over here for this work will be subject to rapid and frequent variations in altitude. It is a common occurrence to dive vertically from six thousand to ten thousand feet with the motor pulling hard.

"Sharpness of vision is imperative. Otherwise the enemy may escape or the aviator himself will be surprised or mistake a friendly machine for a hostile craft. The differences are often merely insignificant colors and details.

"America's aviators must be men who will be absolute masters of themselves under fire, thinking out their attacks as their fight progresses.

"Experience has shown that the 'chaser' men should weigh under one hundred eighty pounds. Americans from the ranks of sport—youths who have played baseball, polo, football, or have shot and participated in other sports—will probably make the best chasers."

Lufbery is a daring aviator and has already been decorated with four military medals awarded for aerial bravery. His life has been full of adventure even before he thought of becoming an airman. *The Ledger* says:

Fifteen years ago the aviator, then seventeen years old, left his home in Wallingford, Conn., and set out to see the world. First he went to France, the land of his progenitors. He visited Paris, Marseilles, Bourges, and other cities. Then he went to Africa.

In Turkey he worked for some time in a restaurant. His plan was to visit a city, get a job that would keep him until he had seen what he desired, and then depart to a new field of adventure. In this manner he traveled through Europe, Africa, and South America. In 1906 he returned to his home in Connecticut. The following year he went to New Orleans, enlisted in the United States army, and was sent to the Philippine Islands. Two years later, upon being mustered out, Lufbery visited Japan and China, exploring those countries thoroughly. Then he went to India and worked as a ticket collector on a Bombay railroad. While engaged at this occupation he kicked out of the railway station one of the most prominent citizens of Bombay. The latter had insisted that Lufbery say "sir" to him. The aviator always did have a hot temper.

Lufbery's next occupation, and the business to which he has remained attached ever since, was had at Saigon, Cochin China, where he met Marc Pourpe, a young French aviator, who was giving flying exhibitions in Asia. He needed an assistant. Lufbery never had seen an airplane, but he applied for the job and got it.

The two men gave exhibitions over the French provinces in Indo-China. After one of these flights the King of Cambodia was so pleased that he presented each aviator with a decoration that entitled him to a guard of honor on the streets of any town within the realm.

Lufbery and Pourpe, now inseparable comrades, went to Paris to get a new airplane. War was declared, and Pourpe volunteered as an aviator. Lufbery, who was anxious to be with his friend, tried also to enlist, but was told that he must enter the Foreign Legion, as he was not a French citizen.

Pourpe was shot to death during one of his wonderful air feats; and, wishing to avenge the death of his friend, Lufbery asked to be trained as an airplane pilot. His request was granted and in the summer of 1916 he went to the front as a member of the American Escadrille. It was on August 4 of that year that he brought down his third enemy plane, and soon afterward was decorated with the Military Medal and the French War Cross, with the following citation:

"Lufbery, Raoul, sergeant with the escadrille No. 124; a model of skill, *sang froid*, and courage. Has distinguished himself by numerous long-distance bombardments and by the daily combats which he delivers to enemy airplanes. On July 31 he attacked at short range a group of four German airplanes. He shot one of them down near our lines. On August 4, 1916, he succeeded in bringing down a second one."

Two or more combats a day in the air came to be a common occurrence with Lufbery, and many times he returned to the base with his machine full of holes and his clothing cut by German bullets.

When Lufbery heard of the death of Kiffin Rockwell he ordered his gasoline tank refilled and soared into the sky, in the hope of avenging the death of his comrade. But no enemy machine was to be found. Of Lufbery's further exploits *The Ledger* says:

During the bombardment of the Mauser factories on October 12, 1916, the intrepid aviator brought down a three-manned *aviatik*. This was counted as his fifth official victory and gained him additional honors. It was during this raid that Norman Prince was mortally wounded.

After the escadrille had moved to the Somme battlefield, Lufbery, on November 9 and 10, brought down two more German planes. These, however, fell too far within their own lines to be placed to his official credit. On December 27, 1916, he nearly lost his life in bringing down his sixth flier of the enemy. Four bullets riddled the machine close to his body. For this victory he received the Cross of the Legion of Honor.

In March of this year he was officially credited with bringing down his seventh German aircraft. The others have been sent hurtling to the earth at different times since then.

Lufbery is a quiet, level-headed man. His particular friend in the Lafayette Escadrille of American fliers is Sergeant Paul Pavelka, who also hails from Connecticut, and who has himself seen quite a bit of the world. Lufbery has his own special methods of attacking enemy airplanes; he is cool, cautious, and brave, and an exceptionally fine shot. When he was a soldier in the United States army he won and held the marksmanship medal of his regiment. He has been cited in army orders twice since August, 1916.

HORSE AND HORSE

An anemic elderly woman, who looked as if she might have as much maternal affection as an incubator, sized up a broad-shouldered cockney who was idly looking into a window on the Strand in London, and in a rasping voice said to him:

"My good man, why aren't you in the trenches? Aren't you willing to do anything for your country?"

Turning around slowly, he looked at her a second and replied contemptuously:

"Move on, you slacker! Where's your war-baby?"

WHY TOMMY JOINED THE CHURCH

"Tommy Atkins" pleaded exemption from church parade on the ground that he was an agnostic. The sergeant-major assumed an expression of innocent interest.

"Don't you believe in the Ten Commandments?" he mildly asked the bold freethinker.

"Not one, sir," was the reply.

"What! Not the rule about keeping the Sabbath?"

"No, sir."

"Ah, well, you're the very man I've been looking for to scrub out the canteen."

LIFE AT THE FRONT

HERE are letters from the boys at the front telling the folks at home of their experiences, humorous, pathetic, and tragic. They present pictures of war life with an intimate touch that brings out all the striking detail. James E. Parshall, of Detroit, is serving with the American ambulance unit in the French army. The Detroit *Saturday Night*, which prints his letter, believes that the "drive" referred to by him was either on the Aisne front or in the Verdun sector. The letter says in part:

Dear People: Sherman was right! I have been debating with myself about what to say in this letter. I think I'll tell you all about it and add that if by the time this reaches you you have heard nothing to the contrary, I am all O. K. You see, we are in a big offensive which will be over in about ten days. As a rule it's not nearly as bad as this.

The day before yesterday we arrived at our base, about seven miles from the lines. It is a little town which has been pretty well shot up, and is shelled now about once a week. In the afternoon one driver from each car was taken up and shown the roads and posts. The coin flopped for me.

The roads to the front run mostly through deep woods. These woods are full of very heavy batteries which are continually shelling the enemy, and, in turn, we are continuously being sought out by the *Boche* gunners. As a result, it's some hot place to drive through. Also, as a result of the continuous shelling, the roads are very bad.

I was so nervous when I started this letter that I had to quit, and this is the first time since then that I have felt like writing. A great deal has happened, but in order not to mix everything up I'll start in where I left off.

Our first post from the base is in a little village which is entirely demolished. It is in a little valley, and the two big marine guns that are stationed there draw a very disquieting *Boche* fire about five times a day regularly. The next post is at a graveyard in the woods. There are no batteries in the immediate vicinity, and so it is quiet, but not very cheerful. (That's where I am now, "on reserve.")

The third post out is where we got our initiation. It was a hot one! Right next to the *abri* is a battery of three very large mortars. Besides these there are several batteries of smaller guns. When we came up they were all going at full tilt. In addition, the *Boches* had just got the range and the shells were exploding all around us. As we jumped out of the car and ran for the *abri* two horses tied to a tree about fifty feet from us were hit and killed. We waited in the *abri* till the bombardment calmed a bit. When we came out two more horses were dead and a third kicking his last.

From here we walked about a half mile to the most advanced post on that road. I'll never forget that walk! The noise was terrific and the shells passing overhead made a continuous scream. Quite frequently we would hear the distinctive screech of an incoming shell. Then everyone would fall flat on his stomach in the road.

Believe me, we were a scared bunch of boys! I was absolutely terrified, and I don't think I was the only one. Well, we eventually got back to the car and to the base.

At twelve o'clock that night the *Boches* started shelling the town. You can't imagine the feeling it gives one in the pit of one's stomach to hear the gun go off in the distance, then the horrible screech of the onrushing shell, and finally the deafening explosion that shakes the plaster down on your cot. Our chiefs were at the outposts, and none of us knew enough to get out and go to the *abri*, so we just lay there shivering and sweating a cold sweat through the whole bombardment. Gosh, but I was a scared boy!

Of a gas attack he writes: "We had to wear those suffocating gas masks for five hours," and then:

About three o'clock in the morning the car ahead of us at the post started out in their masks and in the pitch of blackness with a load. In about a half hour one of the boys on the car staggered back into the *abri*, half gassed, and said that they were in the ditch down in a little valley full of gas. So we had to go down and get their load. Believe me, it was some ticklish and nerve-racking job to transfer three groaning *couches* from a car in the ditch at a perilous angle to ours, in a cloud of gas, and with the shells bursting uncomfortably near quite frequently.

We finally got them in and got started. We got about a half mile farther on to the top of the hill going down into what is known as "Death Valley." In the valley was a sight that was most discouraging. Seven or eight horses were lying in the road, gassed, some of them still kicking. A big *camion* was half in the ditch and half on the road. An ammunition caisson that had tried to get past the blockade by going down through the ditch was stuck there.

Remember that all this was just at the break of dawn, in a cloud of gas, with the French batteries making a continuous roar and an occasional *Boche* shell making every one flop on his stomach.

How we ever got through there I really couldn't tell you. My partner told the Frenchmen who were vainly trying to straighten out the mess that we had a couple of dying men in the car, so they yanked a few horses to one side, drove the *camion* a little farther into the ditch, and, by driving over a horse's head and another one's legs, I got through.

On the whole, I've been quite lucky. Some of the other boys have had some really awful experiences.

About the day after tomorrow we go *en repos*, and it's sure going to seem good to eat and sleep, without getting up and sprinting for an *abri* or throwing one's self, and incidentally a plate of good food, on the ground.

We saw a very interesting thing the other day. We were sitting out in front of our cantonment at the base. About a quarter of a mile from us was one of the big observation balloons or "sausages." Suddenly, from behind a cloud, just above the balloon a *Boche* aeroplane darted out. The *Boche* and the balloonist both fired their machine guns at each other simultaneously. The aeroplane wobbled a little and started to volplane to earth. The balloon burst into flames. The observer dropped about fifty feet, and then his parachute opened and he sailed slowly down. When the *Boche* landed they found him dead with a bullet in his chest. It was quite an exciting sight.

A battle between two planes is quite common, and one can look up at almost any time and see the aircraft bombs bursting around some *Boche* thousands of feet in the air.

At last the "drive" is over, and the letter describes the prisoners, at whose youth he expresses surprise. But they are happy, though nearly starved—happy to be prisoners. The writer says:

I have seen hundreds of *Boche* prisoners, four thousand having been taken in the attack. We see them march past the *poste-de-secours* about half an hour after they have been captured. I have talked with several of them and received lots of interesting information. They are all very happy, but nearly starved. Two slightly wounded ones were brought into the post the other day. A dirty little crust of bread was lying on the ground. They both made a dive for it. They are all awfully young, mostly between seventeen and twenty-one.

One of them told me, among other things, that by next spring Germany would be absolutely finished. A soldier's fare, he said, was one pound of poor bread and one liter of wine a day, except during a heavy attack, when they are given some thin soup. The civilians, he said, were still worse off, especially in the cities.

An Iowa boy, a Y. M. C. A. secretary, who is in the *camion* service in the French army, tells how he arrived in Paris, how he happened to become a soldier of France, and some other interesting details, including the amount of his salary—$1.20 per month! He found the ambulance service—which he had intended to join—crowded, and was told that there would be some delay in getting cars. Even if he did get a car he was told that the chances were against his seeing any action, as he might be attached to an inactive division. He was therefore urged to join the *camion* service—the ammunition truck organization—in which he was assured he would be kept busy day and night as long as he could stand it. There was no camouflage about that. In order to get into this service, one must join the French army, and after thinking the matter over for a few days the Iowa lad "joined" the French colors with a group of American college boys. Here is his letter in part as printed in *Wallace's Farmer*, of Des Moines:

So here I am enrolled as a member of the French army, carrying a French gun, gas mask, and helmet, and eating French army rations. We are paid for our services the sum of $1.20 a month. We underwent a week of intensive training, being drilled in the French manual and army movements, and spending our leisure hours in building roads.

Our sector was active when we arrived at the camp, which is situated a few miles back of the lines; so we were put to work almost immediately. We make two kinds of trips, day trips and night trips; and perhaps if I tell you about my first experience in each it will give you an idea of the character.

We were called at 3:30 A.M., so as to be ready to leave at four o'clock. Our convoy went to the nearby loading station and loaded up with 468 rounds of ammunition for the French "75" guns, which correspond to our three-inch guns. We carted these up to the dumping station near the batteries, and then came back. Nothing exciting happened, and we arrived in camp about 7 P.M. That night I was on guard duty during the last watch, and the following morning we worked our cars. The rough roads and the heavy loads are very hard on the cars as well as on the drivers, so that we must go over the cars every day to keep them in the pink of condition.

That afternoon we got our orders to leave at 4 P.M. We loaded with barbed wire, iron posts, and lumber. The man in charge at the yards warned us that the wind was exactly right for Fritz to send over a bit of gas. So we hung our gas masks about our necks. It takes only thirty seconds for the gas to get in its work on you, and you must be prepared to put on the mask quickly. We started for the front at dark; no lights were allowed. We traveled along screened roads, by columns of artillery wagons, and with infantry moving in every direction, and with staff cars and ambulances dodging in and out for several miles. Finally we turned off on a narrow road which bore the marks of having received a shelling, and went through towns which had been leveled absolutely to the ground by shell fire, and passed an endless chain of dugouts, until we came to our destination.

Most of our cars were unloaded and drawn up on a long, straight road just outside of the station, when our batteries opened up on the Germans. They certainly made some noise. They had not fired many rounds before Fritz began to retaliate, and then it was our turn to worry. His first shells went wild over our heads, but he got the range of the roads on which our trucks were packed, and very soon a shell struck about half a mile down the road. The next shell came closer. He was getting our range and coming straight up the road with his shrapnel.

By this time the remaining cars were unloaded and had swung into line ready to leave. Just as a big shrapnel burst about fifty yards away, our lieutenant gave orders to start, and to start quickly. Believe me, brother, we did! The shells were screaming over our heads, and I was just about scared to death. I should not have worried about the screaming shells, because they are harmless as a barking dog. It is when they stop screaming that you want to get worried.

Then he describes briefly the horrors of the war and expresses some doubt as to man's status being much above that of the beast. He says:

When you see the fields laid waste, depopulated, battered, and desolated, and people in the last stages of poverty, you doubt whether man is nearer to God than is the most cruel of beasts. It is truly a war for liberty, for liberty in politics, ideals, and standards of living. I believe that any one here who is at all sensitive or responsive to his environment feels as I do.

THE "FIDDLER'S TRUCE" AT ARRAS

TWENTY miles away the Prussians and the Canadians were struggling in the dust and mud for the battered suburbs of Lens, but the trenches which were enjoying the "Fiddler's Truce" were not marked to be taken by the staff officers of either army, and the only sign of war was the growling of the big guns far away. Here, too, Canadian opposed Prussian, but they did not fight until the death of Henry Schulman, killed by a most regrettable accident. He was only a private and not sufficiently famous as a violinist to have his death recorded in the musical journals of the world, but along the trenches his taking off is still being discussed as one of the real tragedies of the war.

Late in the fall, after the Somme offensive was over, three Canadian regiments arrived on the Arras front and dug themselves into the brown mud to wait until spring made another advance practicable. Two hundred feet away were three Prussian regiments. There was little real fighting. When the routine of trench life became too monotonous a company would blaze away at the other trenches for a few minutes. At night it was so quiet that conversation in one trench carried over to the other, and there was a good deal of good-natured kidding back and forth. The Canadians were especially pleased by the nightly concerts of the Germans, and applauded heartily the spirited fiddling of one hidden musician. The rest of the story can best be told by Corporal Harry Seaton, in the New York *Evening Mail:*

"One night we held up a piece of white cloth as a sign of truce," he said. "With permission of our colonel I called out and asked the *Boche* if we couldn't have a bit of a concert. It was agreed, and Schulman—that was the fiddler's name—crawled out from his trench. One or two of our Johnnies crawled out, too, just as a sign of good faith.

"Believe me, every one enjoyed the rest of that evening, and when things grew quiet next day somebody yelled for the fiddler to strike up a tune. He was a cobbler in Quebec before the war, and two of our Johnnies knew him and his wife and kids. It didn't take much coaxing after that, and he came out on the strip of 'No Man's Land' and played every night.

"On the 23d of February we were ordered on to another part of the field and another regiment took our old trenches. Of course, in the hurry of departure nobody thought of Schulman.

"That night he brought his stool out as usual, but before he could draw bow across the strings the strangers filled him full of lead. Of course, they didn't know.

"The chaplain told us the story next day and we took up a collection to send back to the family in Berlin. I wonder if they ever got it!"

HARRY LAUDER DOES HIS BIT

THE Y. M. C. A. and Harry Lauder are two social forces that one does not spontaneously connect up. But the former was the agency that brought the singer into the fighting camps of France, not only to hearten the soldiers there, but to pay a touching tribute to the sacrifice of his only son. Dr. George Adam, of Edinburgh, who went with him, gives an account of the trip in *Association Men* (New York), the official organ of the Y. M. C. A. He also speaks of service under the banner of the Red Triangle that Mr. Lauder has rendered which brings the singing comedian before us in a manner hitherto unsuspected:

"On a recent Sunday, although working at full pressure during the week in the play 'Three Cheers' at the Shaftesbury Theater, he gave up his rest day gladly to go away down to two of the great Canadian camps with me.

"Some one in London asked the little man why he was going down to the camps. Why not join them in a quiet week-end on the river? Lauder's reply was as quaint as usual: 'The boys can't get up to town to see me, so I am off to the camps to see them.' A right royal time he gave them, too. Picture ten thousand men in a dell on the rolling downs with a little platform in the center and there Lauder singing the old favorites you have heard so often and the soldiers love so much—'Rocked in the Cradle of the Deep,' 'Bantry Bay,' 'The Laddies Who Fought and Won,' 'Children's Home,' and many more.

"This was not all; his soul must have been stirred by the sight of so many dear, brave men, for when the meeting seemed over, Lauder began to speak to the soldiers. And a real speech he made, full of imagery, poetry, and fire. May I just tell you how he closed? 'One evening in the gloaming in a northern town I was sitting by my parlor window when I saw an old man with a pole on his shoulder come along. He was a lamp-lighter, and made the lamp opposite my window dance into brightness. Interested in his work, I watched him pass along until the gloaming gathered round and I could see him no more. However, I knew just where he was, for other lamps flashed into flame. Having completed his task, he disappeared into a side street. Those lamps burned on through the night, making it bright and safe for those who should come behind him. An avenue of lights through the traffic and dangers of the city.'

"With passionate earnestness Lauder cried: 'Boys, think of that man who lit the lamp, for you are his successors, only in a much nobler and grander way. You are not lighting for a few hours the darkness of passing night. You are lighting an avenue of lights that will make it safe for the generations of all time. Therefore, you must be earnest to do the right. Fight well and hard against every enemy without and within, and those of your blood who come after you will look up proudly in that light of freedom and say, "The sire that went before me lit a lamp in those heroic days when Britain warred for right." The first burst of illumination that the world had was in the lamp lit by Jesus, or rather he was the Light himself. He said truly, "I am the Light of the world." You are in his succession. Be careful how you bear yourselves. Quit ye like men! Be strong!'"

The story of the effort made to induce the singing comedian to go "out there" touches on his well-known human frailty, in this case triumphantly overcome:

"During a visit to France, and in conversation with one in high command in the army, talk turned to the high place Lauder had in the affections of his countrymen, for we were both Scots. A strong desire was expressed that he should be got out among the soldiers in the battle line just to give them the cheer he knows so well how to impart. I promised to endeavor to arrange it, with trepidation, you may be sure, for you know what is so often said of Lauder and his money. However, with courage in both hands I asked him to give up the week that meant many thousands of dollars to go out to the boys.

"The request seemed to stagger him, and for a minute I felt I was to fail, but it was the good fortune to receive such a request that took his breath away. 'Give me a week's notice and I go with you, and glad to go.' I replied, 'I give you notice now.' Whereupon he called to his manager, 'Tom, I quit in a week'; and he did, and off to the war zone he went. My pen is unequal to the task of describing that wonderful tour and the amazing results of it. The men went wild with enthusiasm and joy wherever he went. One great meeting was apparently seen by some German airmen, who communicated the information to one of their batteries of artillery. In the middle of a song—whiz, bang!—went a big shell very close at hand—so close, in fact, that pieces struck but a foot or two from where we both stood. There was a scatter and a scamper for cover, and for three-quarters of an hour the Huns hammered the position with two hundred big ones. When the bombardment ended, Lauder of the big-hearted Scotch courage must needs finish his concert."

Another incident shows the heart of Harry Lauder as those who have only heard his rollicking songs will rejoice in.

"One day during our visit I was taking Harry to see the grave of his only child, Capt. John Lauder, of the Argyle and Sutherland Highlanders, as fine a lad as ever wore a kilt, and as good and brave a son as ever a father loved. As we were motoring swiftly along we turned into the town of Albert and the first sharp glance at the cathedral showed the falling Madonna and Child. It was a startling and arresting sight, and we got out to have a good look. The building is crowned by a statue of Mary holding out the child Jesus to the world; a German shell had struck its base and it fell over, not to the ground, however, but at an acute angle out over the street.

"While we lingered, a bunch of soldiers came marching through, dusty and tired. Lauder asked the officer to halt his men for a rest and he would sing to them. I could see that they were loath to believe it was the real Lauder until he began to sing.

"Then the doubts vanished and they abandoned themselves to the full enjoyment of this very unexpected pleasure. When the singsong began the audience would number about two hundred; at the finish of it easily more than two thousand soldiers cheered him on his way.

"It was a strange send-off on the way that led to a grave—the grave of a father's fondest hopes—but so it was. A little way up the Bapaume road the car stopped and we clambered the embankment and away over the shell-torn field of Courcelette. Here and there we passed a little cross which marked the grave of some unknown hero; all that was written was 'A British Soldier.' He spoke in a low voice of the hope-hungry hearts behind all those at home. Now we climbed a little ridge and here a cemetery and in the first row facing the battlefield the cross on Lauder's boy's resting-place.

"The father leaned over the grave to read what was written there. He knelt down; indeed, he lay upon the grave and clutched it, the while his body shook with the grief he felt.

"When the storm had spent itself he rose and prayed: 'O God, that I could have but one request. It would be that I might embrace my laddie just this once and thank him for what he has done for his country and humanity.'

"That was all, not a word of bitterness or complaint.

"On the way down the hill I suggested gently that the stress of such an hour made further song that day impossible.

"But Lauder's heart is big and British. Turning to me with a flash in his eye he said: 'George, I must be brave; my boy is watching and all the other boys are waiting. I will sing to them this afternoon though my heart break!' Off we went again to another division of Scottish troops.

"There, within the hour, he sang again the sweet old songs of love and home and country, bringing all very near and helping the men to realize the deeper what victory for the enemy would mean. Grim and determined men they were that went back to their dugouts and trenches, heartened for the task of war for human freedom by Harry Lauder. Harry's little kilted figure came and went from the war zone, but his influence remains, the influence of a heroic heart."

CAUSE FOR GRIEVANCE

A wounded soldier explained his grievance to his nurse:

"You see, old Smith was next to me in the trenches. Now, the bullet that took me in the shoulder and laid me out went into 'im and made a bit of a flesh-wound in his arm. Of course I'm glad he wasn't 'urt bad. But he's stuck to my bullet and given it his girl. Now, I don't think that's fair. I'd a right to it. I'd never give a girl 'o mine a second-'and bullet."

DOUBLY ANNOYING

A German spy caught redhanded was on his way to be shot.

"I think you English are brutes," he growled, "to march me through this rain and slush."

"Well," said the "Tommy" who was escorting him, "what about me? I have to go back in it."

KING GEORGE UNDER FIRE

KING GEORGE and Queen Mary have been seeing war at close range. Together they made an eleven days' visit to the British troops in France, and while there the King experienced the sensation of being under fire. While the Queen devoted herself to the hospitals and the sick and wounded, the King was shown all the latest devices for killing and maiming the enemy. It was soon after seeing what would happen to the Teutons that he decided to drop his Teutonic name and become Mr. Windsor. Says a dispatch from the British headquarters in the New York *Sun:*

On the first morning after his arrival in France, King George visited the Messines Ridge sector of the front, climbing the ridge while the Germans were shelling the woods just to his left. He inspected the ground over which the Irish troops, men from the north and the south, fought so gallantly side by side during the taking of the Messines Ridge, and where Major William Redmond fell. While the King was doing this the Germans began shelling places on the ridge which he had left but half an hour before. The King visited also Vimy Ridge, from which he could see the German lines about Lens, with British shells breaking on them.

For the benefit of the King a special show was staged that he might witness "that black art of frightfulness which has steadily increased the horrors of war since the day when the enemy let loose clouds of poisoned gas upon the soldiers and civilians in Ypres," says Philip Gibbs in the Philadelphia *Public Ledger:*

As soon as the King arrived on the field there was a sound of rushing air, and there shot forth a blast of red flame out of black smoke to a great distance and with a most terrifying effect. It came from an improved variety of flame projector. Then the King saw the projection of burning oil, burst out in great waves of liquid fire. A battalion of men would be charred like burned sticks if this touched them for a second. There was another hissing noise, and there rolled very sluggishly over the field a thick, oily vapor, almost invisible as it mixed with the air, and carrying instant death to any man who should take a gulp of it. To such a thing have all of us come in this war for civilization.

The most spectacular show here was the most harmless to human life, being a new form of smoke barrage to conceal the movement of troops on the battlefield.

From this laboratory of the black art the King went to one of those fields where the machinery of war is beautiful, rising above the ugly things of this poor earth with light and grace, for this was an air-drome. As he came up, three fighting planes of the fastest British type went up in chase of an imaginary enemy. They arose at an amazing speed and shot across the sky-line like shadows racing from the sun. When they came back those three boys up there seemed to go a little mad and played tricks in the air with a kind of joyous carelessness of death. They tumbled over and over, came hurtling down in visible corkscrews, looped the loop very close to the earth, flattened out after headlong dives, and rose again like swallows. The King was interested in the ages of these pilots and laughed when they confessed their youth, for one was nineteen and another twenty.

The antics of the "tanks" furnished the King with a great deal of amusement. Leaving the air-drome, he was driven to a sunken field, very smooth and long, between two high wooded banks. Says Mr. Gibbs:

Here there was a great surprise and a great sensation, for just as the King stepped out of his car a young tree in full foliage on the left of the field up a high bank toppled forward slowly and then fell with a crash into the undergrowth. Something was moving in the undergrowth, something monstrous. It came heaving and tearing its way through the bushes, snapping off low branches and smashing young saplings like an elephant on stampede. Then it came into sight on top of the bank, a big gray beast, with a blunt snout, nosing its way forward and all tangled in green leaves and twigs. It was old brother tank doing his stunt before the King.

From the far end of a long, smooth field came two other twin beasts of this ilk, crawling forward in a hurry as though hungry for human blood. In front of their track, at the other end of the field, were two breastworks built of sand-bags covering some timbered dugouts and protected from sudden attack by two belts of barbed wire. The two tanks came along like hippopotamuses on a spree, one of them waiting for the other when he lagged a little behind. They hesitated for a moment before the breastworks as if disliking the effort of climbing them, then heaved themselves up, thrust out their snouts, got their hind quarters on the move, and waddled to the top. Under their vast weight the sand-bags flattened out, the timber beneath slipped and cracked, and the whole structure began to collapse, and the twins plunged down on the other side and advanced to attack the barbed wire.

Another tank now came into action from the far end of the field, bearing the legend on its breast of "*Faugh-a-ballagh*," which, I am told, is Irish for "get out of the way." It was the Derby winner of the tanks' fleet. From its steel flanks guns waggled to and fro, and no dragon of old renown looked half so menacing as this. St. George would have had no chance against it. But King George, whose servant it was, was not afraid, and with the Prince of Wales he went through the steel trap-door into the body of the beast. For some time we lost sight of the King and Prince, but after a while they came out laughing, having traveled around the field for ten minutes in the queerest car on earth.

The great thrill of the day came later. Through the woods of a high bank on the left came a tank, looking rather worse for wear, as though battered in battle.

It came forward through the undergrowth and made for the edge of the bank, where there was a machine gun emplacement in a bomb-proof shelter, whose steep bank was almost perpendicular. It seemed impossible that any old tank should entertain a notion of taking that jump, but this tank came steadily on until its snout was well over the bank and steadily on again with that extraordinary method of progression in which the whole body of the beast moves from the nose end upward until it seems to have a giraffe's neck and very little else. That very little else was sitting on the top of the emplacement while the forward part of the tank was poised in space regarding the setting sun. However, without any hesitation, the whole mass moved on, lurched out, and nose-dived.

Good Lord! it was then that the thrill came. The tank plunged down like a chunk of cliff as it fell, went sideways and lost its balance, and, as near as anything could be, almost turned turtle. It righted itself with a great jerk at the nick of time just before it took the earth below and shaved by a hair's breadth an ammunition dump at the bottom of the drop.

It was the finest tank trick I ever saw, and it was greeted with laughter and cheers. The King, however, and other spectators were rather worried about the lads inside. They must have taken a mighty toss. No sound came from the inside of the tank, and for a moment some of us had a vision of a number of plucky fellows laid out unconscious within those steel walls. The door opened and we could see their feet standing straight, which was a relief.

"Let them all come out," said the King, laughing heartily. And out they all tumbled, a row of young fellows as merry and bright as air pilots after a good landing.

THE FEMALE STANDARD OF SIZE

Lady (entering bank, very businesslike)—"I wish to get a Liberty Loan bond for my husband."

Clerk—"What size, please?"

Lady—"Why, I don't believe I know, exactly, but he wears a fifteen shirt."

STORY OF OUR FIRST SHOT

"I PICKED that shell right up as it came out of the gun—I saw it go through the air in its flight, and I saw it strike a foot in front of that periscope!"

That is the way Lieut. Bruce R. Ware, Jr., U. S. N., who commanded the gun crew of the steamship *Mongolia*, told of the first American shot fired in the war at a German submarine. He related the story at a testimonial dinner given to him and to Capt. Emery Rice, of the *Mongolia*, upon the arrival of the steamship at New York. The dinner was attended by many persons prominent in business, steamship, and naval circles, some having traveled hundreds of miles to be present. As reported by the New York *Times*, Lieutenant Ware told the story as follows:

At 5:21 the chief officer walked out on the port bridge. The captain and myself were on our heels looking out through the port. I saw the chief officer turn around, and you could have seen the whole ocean written in his face, and his mouth that wide (indicating), and he could not get it out. He finally said: "My God, look at that submarine!"

The captain gripped my arm and said: "What is that?" I said: "It is a submarine, and he has got up."

I followed the captain out on the bridge and I looked at my gun crews. They were all agape. The lookout was all agape. I threw in my starboard control and I said: "Captain, zigzag." I did not tell him which way to go. We had that all doped out. The captain starboarded his helm and the ship turned to port and we charged him (the *U*-boat) and made him go under. I went up on top of the chart house with my phones on, and I had a long, powerful glass, ten power. Right underneath it I always lashed my transmitter, so that where I was my transmitter went, and I didn't have to worry or hunt for it. It was always plugged in, and I said:

"No. 3 gun, after gun, train on the starboard quarter, and when you see a submarine and periscope or conning tower, report."

The gun crew reported control. "We see it—no, no—it has gone. There it is again." I picked it up at that moment with my high-powered glass, and I gave them the range—1,000 yards. Scale 50. She was about 800 yards away from us. I gave the order, "No. 3 gun, fire, commence firing."

I had my glasses on them, gentlemen, and I saw that periscope come up. "No. 3 gun, commence firing, fire, fire, fire." And they did, and I picked that shell right up as it came out of the gun—a black, six-inch explosive shell. I saw it go through the air in its flight, and I saw it strike the water eight inches—a foot—in front of that periscope and it went into the conning tower. I saw that periscope go end over end, whipping through that water, and I saw plates go off his conning tower, and I saw smoke all over the scene where we had hit the enemy.

When Captain Rice was called upon for a speech he said:

"Gentlemen, I'd much rather take the *Mongolia* through the war zone than make a speech. All I will say is that I am ready to go again, and I hope I have another chance at a *U*-boat."

HE KNEW WHAT TO DO

A short time back, while a certain general was inspecting a regiment just about to depart for new quarters, he asked a young subaltern what would be his next order if he was in command of a regiment passing over a plain in a hostile country, and he found his front blocked by artillery, a brigade of cavalry on his right flank, and a morass on his left, while his retreat was cut off by a large body of infantry.

"Halt! Order arms, ground arms, kneel down, say your prayers!" replied the subaltern.

THAT WAS THE HYMN NUMBER

Here is a story which if it is not true ought to be. The soldier in the train was dilating on his changed life.

"They took me from my home," he said, "and put me in barracks; they took away my clothes and put me in khaki; they took away my name and made me 'No. 575'; they took me to church, where I'd never been before, and they made me listen to a sermon for forty minutes. Then the parson said, 'No. 575, Art thou weary, art thou languid?' And I got seven days' C.B. for giving him a civil answer."

STORIES FROM THE FRONT

INTIMATE stories of life in the trenches "somewhere in France" are told in two letters that describe in man-to-man fashion incidents that present an unusual picture of the battle front, full of color as well as of darkening shadows. The letters were written by Mr. Stevenson P. Lewis, serving with the American Ambulance Corps, to his cousin, Mr. W. O. Curtiss, of Toledo, Ohio. They are dated May 21 and 26, and extracts are printed in the Toledo *Blade*. Mr. Lewis has no complaint to make of the food. He finds the horse meat "a little tough," but seemingly palatable. He writes:

We get good food, but miss the extra dishes. We get the famous army bread, rather sour taste, but am used to it now—no butter, of course; oatmeal without milk or sugar, horse meat, potatoes, and various flavors of jam. The horse meat is usually a little tough, but otherwise pretty good. Have biscuits and chocolate at the canteen. A couple of pieces of hardtack, with water and chocolate, do for a dinner very well when away from camp.

We have considerable time just now, with nothing to fill in, and I can't quite go it, so I hike out for walks and have picked up quite a few good pictures and souvenirs. Picked up an eagle with spread wings—German silver, a decoration worn on a German officer's helmet, inscribed "*Mitt Gott für König und Vaterland*." It is rather a rare find, as the old spiked helmet is not worn any more.

Sunday we had a visit from Germany in the shape of an airplane which dropped five bombs in the next village. Two French machines gave chase and brought him down, but he caused considerable excitement until he reached the ground. They always come over at a high altitude and do not seem in any hurry to leave, regardless of the shrapnel shots placed around the planes. This one, the second we have seen come down, made two complete turns and then dived straight down.

We have had some trouble with some of the men in charge, due to the wandering of one of our men into the first line trenches. The man guilty has acted ever since he arrived as though missing in essential brain cells, but this time he crowned his former efforts—walked up a valley with *Boche* trenches on one side, French on the other, he down the middle in No Man's Land. Lucky he came back at all. The French called him over to their trenches, otherwise I suppose he would be walking into Berlin by this time.

We are working with an English ambulance section, taking turns making runs to field stations, where the wounded are sent direct from trenches. We carry them from these first-aid posts back to another post, and the English section, with its large cars, carry them ten or fifteen miles farther back. Then the order is reversed. The English are a mighty interesting lot, and most of them have been in service since 1914, hence have seen action all along this front. The hardest driving is at night running up to the posts just back of the lines, for all the moving is done then. The road is crowded with ammunition trucks, supplies, guns, and troops, and with no lights it is uncertain what is coming or going. Several men have ditched their cars and run by the station, but no serious accidents have occurred. Star shells sent up at intervals give a blinding light and the whole country-side is as light as day for a short time, then suddenly dark. It is this quick change that makes it hard to adjust our vision.

This English section has been through the hottest fighting on this front, having been posted at Verdun last year and running to the most advanced posts, but never lost a man and had only a few slight accidents. A person would think they were playing a safe game, but not so, after hearing of some bombardments they ran through. One man in the British ambulance corps has the Victoria Cross, the hardest war medal of any to get. He drove his car up the lines in plain sight of the Germans. One of the stretcher bearers having been killed, he rushed out on to No Man's Land with another man and rescued several men, put them into his car, and drove off, all the time being the object of German fire.

The English are world-beaters in the flying game, as I suppose you have heard. The minute a *Boche* plane appears over their lines, a couple of fast monoplanes are after it and usually bring it down. Heard of one air battle between five English machines and ten Germans; five of the German machines were brought down and the remaining five headed for Berlin with two English planes after them. The English did not lose a machine. Again there were three German "sausages" (observation balloons), and three English aviators, each in a machine, were detailed to bring them down, each aviator to take a balloon. Two of the Englishmen each got their balloon, but the Germans, seeing what had happened, lowered the third balloon. However, the Englishman ordered to get it, being ruffled a bit because he did not get a chance to get his "bag" as the other two did, dived down over the balloon resting in German territory, setting it afire and killing a number of Germans. He was wounded badly, but succeeded in bringing his machine back. He was awarded the Victoria Cross. Many other war medals are given, but a man who gets the Victoria Cross really has done a feat of individual bravery.

FUNNY THEY HADN'T MET

Pretty Lady Visitor (at private hospital)—"Can I see Lieutenant Barker, please?"

Matron—"We do not allow ordinary visiting. May I ask if you're a relative?"

Visitor (boldly)—"Oh, yes! I'm his sister."

Matron—"Dear me! I'm very glad to meet you. I'm his mother."

NO END TO THE GAME

Two American lads were discussing the war.

"It'll be an awful long job, Sam," said one.

"It will," replied the other.

"You see, these Germans is takin' thousands and thousands of Russian prisoners, and the Russians is takin' thousands and thousands of German prisoners. If it keeps on, all the Russians will be in Germany and all the Germans in Russia. And then they'll start all over again, fightin' to get back their 'omes."

UNCLE SAM, DETECTIVE

THE detective work accomplished by the United States Government since its entry into the war has been worthy of a Sherlock Holmes, and yet few persons, reading only the results of this remarkably developed system, have realized that a Government heretofore finding it unnecessary to match wits with foreign spy bureaus has suddenly taken a high rank in this unpleasant but absolutely essential branch of war-making—as it has in all others. The public read of the intercepted dispatches from the Argentine to Germany by way of Sweden, and of the Bernstorff messages, but without a realization of the problem that a cipher dispatch presents to one who has not the key. And probably the average reader is unaware that, in both the army and navy, experts have been trained to decipher code messages, with the result that both the making and the reading of such dispatches have been reduced to an almost mathematical science. The Philadelphia *Press*, in outlining the instruction given in this important work at the Army Service schools, says:

What is taught the military will furnish an idea of the task of the code experts in the State Department, and of the basis of the science that has unmasked the German plans with respect to vessels to be *spurlos versenkt* and of legislators to be influenced through the power of German gold.

"It may as well be stated," says Capt. Parker Hitt—that is, he was a captain of infantry when he said it—"that no practicable military cipher is mathematically indecipherable if intercepted; the most that can be expected is to delay for a longer or shorter time the deciphering of the message by the interceptor."

The young officer is warned that one doesn't have to rely in these times upon capturing messengers as they speed by horse from post to post. All radio messages may be picked up by every operator within the zone, and the interesting information is given that if one can run a fine wire within one hundred feet of a buzzer line or within thirty feet of a telegraph line, whatever tidings may be going over these mediums may be copied by induction.

In order that the student may not lose heart, it is pointed out in the beginning that many European powers use ciphers that vary from extreme simplicity to "a complexity which is more apparent than real." And as to amateurs, who make up ciphers for some special purpose, it's dollars to doughnuts that their messages will be read just as easily as though they had printed them in box-car letters.

At every headquarters of an army the intelligence department of the General Staff stands ready to play checkers with any formidable looking document that comes along in cipher, and there is mighty little matter in code that stands a ghost of a chance of getting by.

The scientific dissection of ciphers starts with the examination of the general system of language communication, which, with everybody excepting friend Chinaman, is an alphabet composed of letters that appear in conventional order.

It was early found by the keen-eyed gentlemen who analyzed ciphers that if one took ten thousand words of any language and counted the letters in them the number of times that any one letter would recur would be found practically identical with their recurrence in any other ten thousand words. From this discovery the experts made frequency tables, which show just how many times one may expect to find a letter e or any other letter in a given number of words or letters. These tables were made for ten thousand letters and for two hundred letters, so that one might get an idea how often to expect to find given letters in both long and short messages or documents.

Thus we find the following result:

Letters

	100 00	2 00
/	778	16
ꞁ	141	3
(	296	6
ꞁ	402	8

	1277	26
	197	4
	174	3
	595	12
	667	13
	51	1
	74	2
	372	7
	288	6
	686	14
	807	16
	223	4
	8	..
	651	13
	622	12
	855	17
	308	6
	112	2
	176	3
	27	..
	196	4
	17	..

It is found that in any text the vowels A E I O U represent 38.37 per cent; that the consonants L N R S T represent 31.86 per cent, and that the consonants J K Q X Z stand for only 1.77 per cent. One doesn't want to shy away from these figures as being dry and dull, because they form part of a story as interesting as any detective narrative that was ever penned by a Conan Doyle.

For the usual purposes of figuring a cipher the first group is given the value of 40 per cent, the second group 30 per cent, and the last 2 per cent. And then one is introduced to the order of frequency in which letters appear in ordinary text. It is:

E T O A N I R S H D L U C M P F Y W G B V K J X Z Q.

Tables are then made for kinds of matter that is not ordinary, taken from various kinds of telegraphic and other documents, which will alter only slightly the percentage values of the letters as shown in a table from ordinary English.

Having gone along thus far, the expert figures how many times he can expect to find two letters occurring together. These are called digraphs, and one learns that AH will show up once in a thousand letters, while HA will be found twenty-six times. These double-letter combinations form a separate table all of their own, and the common ones are set aside, as TH, ER, ON, OR, etc., so they can be readily guessed or mathematically figured against any text.

Tables of frequency are figured out for the various languages, particularly German, and the ciphers are divided into two chief classes, substitution and transposition. The writer in *The Press* says:

Now you will remember those percentages of vowels and consonants. Here is where they come in. When a message is picked up the army expert counts the times that the vowels recur, and if they do not check with the 40 per cent for the common vowels, with the consonant figures tallying within 5 per cent of the key, he knows that he is up against a substitution cipher. The transposition kind will check to a gnat's heel.

When the expert knows exactly what he is up against he is ready to apply the figures and patiently unravel the story. It may take him hours, and maybe days, but sooner or later he will get it to a certainty.

If he has picked up a transposition fellow he proceeds to examine it geometrically, placing the letters so that they form all sorts of squares and rectangles that come under the heads of simple horizontals, simple verticals, alternate horizontals, alternate verticals, simple diagonals, alternate diagonals, spirals reading clockwise, and spirals reading counter-clockwise. Once one gets the arrangement of the letters, the reading is simple.

For instance, ILVGIOIAEITSRNMANHMNG comes along the wire. It doesn't figure for a substitution cipher and you try the transposition plan. There are twenty-one letters in it, and the number at once suggests seven columns of three letters each. Try it on your piano:

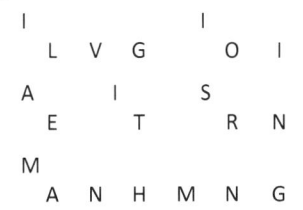

```
I           I
  L  V  G     O  I
A    I     S
  E     T     R  N
M
  A  N  H  M  N  G
```

And reading down each column in succession you get "I am leaving this morning."

After passing over several simple ciphers as not "classy" enough to engage the reader's attention, the writer takes up one of a much more complicated nature, which, however, did not get by Uncle Sam's code wizards. Follow the deciphering of this example by Captain Hitt:

He began with an advertisement which appeared in a London newspaper, which read as follows:

"M. B. Will deposit £27 14s. 5d. to-morrow."

The next day this advertisement in cipher appeared:

"M. B. CT OSB UHGI TP IPEWF H CEWIL NSTTLE FJNVX XTYLS FWKKHI BJLSI SQ VOI BKSM XMKUL SK NVPONPN GSW OL IEAG NPSI HYJISFZ CYY NPUXQG TPRJA VXMXI AP EHVPPR TH WPPNEL. UVZUA MMYVSF KNTS ZSZ UAJPQ DLMMJXL JR RA PORTELOGJ CSULTWNI XMKUHW XGLN ELCPOWY OL. ULJTL BVJ TLBWTPZ XLD K ZISZNK OSY DL RYJUAJSSGK. TLFNS UVD W FQGCYL FJHVSI YJL NEXV PO WTOL PYYYHSH GQBOH AGZTIQ EYFAX YPMP SQA CI XEYVXNPPAII UV TLFTWMC FU WBWXGUHIWU. AIIWG HSI YJVTI BJV XMQN SFX DQB LRTY TZ QTXLNISVZ. GIFT AII UQSJGJ OHZ XFOWFV BXAI CTWY DSWTLTTTPKFRHG IVX QCAFV TP DIIS JBF ESF JSC MCCF HNGK ESBP DJPQ NLU CTW ROSB CSM."

Now just off-hand, the average man would shy away from this combination as a bit of news that he really did not care to read. But to the cipher fiend it was a thing of joy, and it illustrates one of the many cases that they are called upon to read, and the methods by which they work.

As a starting-point the cipher-man assumed that the text was in English because he got it out of an English newspaper, but he did not stop there. He checked it from a negative view-point by finding the letter *w* in it, which does not occur in the Latin languages, and

Stories from the Trenches

by finding that the last fifteen words of the message had from two to four letters each, which would have been impossible in German.

Then he proceeds to analyze. The message has 108 groups that are presumably words, and there are 473 letters in it. This makes an average of 4.4 letters to the group, whereas one versed in the art normally expects about five. There are ninety vowels of the AEIOU group and seventy-eight letters JKQXZ. Harking back to that first statement of percentages, it is certain that this is a substitution cipher because the percentage does not check with the transposition averages.

The canny man with the sharp pencil then looks for recurring groups and similar groups in his message and he finds that they are:

AIIWG AII BKSM BKAI CT CTWY CTW DLMMJXL DL ESF ESBP FJNVX FJHVSI NPSI NPUXQG OSB OSY ROSB OL OL PORTELOGJ PO SQ SQA TP TP TLBWTPZ TLFNS TLFTWMC UVZUA UVD UV SMKUL XMKUHW YJL YJVTI.

Passing along by the elimination route he refers to his frequency tables to see how often the same letters occur, and he finds that they are all out of proportion, and he can proceed to hunt the key for several alphabets.

He factors the recurring groups like a small boy doing a sum in arithmetic when he wants to find out how many numbers multiplied by each other will produce a larger one. The number of letters between recurring groups and words is counted and dissected in this wise:

AII	AII	45,	which equals 3x3x5
BK	BK	345,	which equals 23x3x5
CT	CT	403,	no factors
CTW	CTW	60,	which equals 2x2x2x5
DL	DL	75,	which equals 3x5x5
ES	ES	14,	which equals 2x7
FJ	FJ	187,	no factors
NP	NP	14,	which equals 2x7
OL	OL	120,	which equals 2x2x2x3x5
OS	OS	220,	which equals 11x2x2x5
OSB	OSB	465,	which equals 31x3x5
PO	PO	105,	which equals 7x3x5
SQ	SQ	2	which equals 2x5x5x5

38

TLF	TLF	80,	which equals 2x2x2x2x5
TP	TP	405,	which equals 3x3x3x3x5
UV	UV	115,	which equals 23x5
XMKU	XMKU	120,	which equals 2x2x2x3x5
UV	UV	73,	no factors
YJ	YJ	85,	which equals 17x5

Now the man who is doing the studying takes a squint at this result and he sees that the dominant factor all through the case is the figure 5, so he is reasonably sure that five alphabets were used, and that the key-word had, therefore, five letters, so he writes the message in lines of five letters each and makes a frequency table for each one of the five columns he has formed, and he gets the following result:

Col. 1.	Col. 2.	Col. 3.	Col. 4.	Col. 5.
A 2	A 9	A 1	A 1	A 2
B—	B 3	B 3	B—	B 7
C 7	C 1	C 3	C 4	C—
D 2	D 2	D 1	D—	D 3
E 4	E—	E 2	E 7	E—
F 3	F—	F 9	F 3	F 5
G 9	G—	G 3	G 2	G 2
H 3	H 5	H 3	H 3	H 2
I 2	I 2	I 7	I 17	I 2
J 5	J 1	J 6	J—	J 9
K 6	K 5	K—	K 1	K 1
L—	L 19	L 2	L 5	L 1
M—	M—	M 7	M 4	M 3
N 7	N 3	N 4	N—	N 5
O 5	O—	O 9	O 1	O—
P 7	P 7	P 8	P 4	P—
Q 5	Q—	Q—	Q 2	Q 6
R—	R 1	R 1	R 6	R 1
S—	S 8	S 6	S 12	S 7
T 7	T 3	T 5	T 1	T 14

U 7	U 3	U 6	U —	U 1
V 5	V —	V 2	V 5	V —
W 3	W 4	W —	W 5	W 7
X 2	X —	X 4	X 8	X 6
Y 4	Y 5	Y —	Y 3	Y 7
Z —	Z 5	Z 3	Z —	Z 3

Now, having erected these five enigmatical columns, Captain Hitt juggles them until he uncovers the hidden message, thus:

"In the table for column 1 the letter G occurs 9 times," he says with an air of a man having found something that is perfectly plain. "Let us consider it tentatively as E.

"Then, if the cipher alphabet runs regularly and in the direction of the regular alphabet, C (7 times) is equal to A, and the cipher alphabet bears a close resemblance to the regular frequency table. Note that TUV (equal to RST) occurring respectively 7, 7, and 5 times and the non-occurrence of B, L, M, R, S, Z (equal to Z, J, K, P, Q, and X, respectively).

"In the next table L occurs 19 times, and taking it for E with the alphabet running the same way, A is equal to H. The first word of our message, CT, thus becomes AM when deciphered with these two alphabets, and the first two letters of the key are CH.

"Similarly in the third table we may take either F or O for E, but a casual examination shows that the former is correct and A is equal to B.

"In the fourth table I is clearly E and A is equal to E.

"The fifth table shows that T is equal to 14 and J is equal to 9. If we take J as equal to E then T is equal to O, and in view of the many Es already accounted for in the other columns this may be all right. It checks as correct if we apply the last three alphabets to the second word of our message, OSB, which deciphers NOW. Using these alphabets to decipher the whole message we find it to read:

"'M. B. Am now safe on board a barge moored below Tower Bridge, where no one will think of looking for me. Have good friends but little money owing to action of police. Trust, little girl, you still believe in my innocence although things seem against me. There are reasons why I should not be questioned. Shall try to embark before the mast in some outward-bound vessel. Crews will not be scrutinized as sharply as passengers. There are those who will let you know my movements. Fear the police may tamper with your correspondence, but later on, when hue and cry have died down, will let you know all.'"

It all seems simple to the man who follows the idea closely, but Captain Hitt proceeds to make further revelations of the art. He adds:

"The key to this message is CHBEF, which is not intelligible as a word, but if put into figures, indicating that the 2d, 7th, 1st, 4th, and 5th letter beyond the corresponding letter of the message has been used as a key it becomes 27145, and we connect it with the personal which appeared in the same paper the day before reading:

"'M. B. Will deposit £27 14s. 5d. tomorrow.'"

This is only one of the many methods for getting under the hide of a coded message that our bright men of the Army and their cousins of the State and Navy departments have worked out through years of study and application.

DRIVING IS TOO GOOD FOR THEM

He—"And that night we drove the Germans back two miles."

She—"Drove them, indeed. I'd have made them walk every step of it."

NOW THEY DON'T SPEAK

The Host—"I thought of sending some of these cigars out to the Front."

The Victim—"Good idea! But how can you make certain that the Germans will get them?"

DIDN'T RAISE HIS BOY TO BE A "SLACKER"

THEY don't raise their boys to be gun-shy down in the mountains of Kentucky, so when John Calhoun Allen, of Clay County, heard that his son had been arrested in New York as a "slacker" he was "plumb mad."

The young man was rounded up with a bunch of other "conscientious objectors" and taken before Judge Mayer in the Federal Court. John C. junior told the judge that during his boyhood in the Kentucky mountains he had witnessed so much bloodshed that he was now opposed to fighting and had a horror of killing a man or, in fact, of being killed himself. The judge was puzzled. He had never heard before of a Kentuckian with any such complaint, so he packed the young man off to Bellevue for the "once-over" while he communicated the facts to his father down in Clay County, and, says the New York *Times:*

The answer arrived in the form of the 6 feet 2 inches of John Allen himself. The mountaineer came into court just before the noon hour. He wore the boots and the corduroy trousers of the Kentucky hills. His shirt was blue, collarless, and home-made. His coat was old-fashioned, and in his hand he carried his big black sombrero.

"May it please your honor," said United States District Attorney Knox, "we have with us the father of John Calhoun Allen."

The mountaineer looked the Judge squarely in the eye and bowed. Tall and erect, he towered above every other man in the court room and he was not in the least embarrassed.

"Judge," he said, "I got your letter and I thank you for it, and I started to answer it in writin', but decided that maybe it was better that I come here myself and see what's the matter with that boy of mine. It ain't like our folks to act as that youngster has acted, and I assure you that I am plumb mad about it. I have five boys, and this one who is in trouble here is the oldest. Two of my lads are already in the Army and the two youngest will be there soon as they are old enough.

"And so I have come all the way from Kentucky to get this one who I hear is a backslider. All I ask is for you to let me take my boy back to Kentucky with me, and I will see to it that he comes to time when his country calls. There ain't going to be no quitters in the Allen family. My boys that are already in the Army ain't twenty-one yet. This one is my oldest and he's the first to miss the trail, but he'll find the trail again or I'll know the reason why."

"I have the utmost confidence in you," said Judge Mayer after the old man finished, "and I shall release your son in your custody, confident that you will see to it that he obeys the law and registers."

"He'll register all right, Judge," replied the old man, "and I tell you that if he don't, something will happen in the public square back home, and all the folks will have a chance to see with their own eyes that the Allens don't stand for no quitters at a time when the country needs all the men it can get."

In the meantime Marshal McCarthy had sent to the Tombs for young Allen, and the young man was waiting in the Marshal's office when his father arrived. They are self-contained people down in the Kentucky mountains. Their feelings are deep, but well controlled, so that when father and son met there was no show of emotion on the part of either. But the sight of his son softened the father's anger. He placed his hand gently on the younger man's shoulder, and this is the way *The Times* describes the scene that followed:

"Son," said the father, "don't you know what it means to do what you tried to do? Don't you know that you don't come from no such stock as these slackers and quitters, or whatever else you call such cattle? Don't you know that, boy? Well, if you don't, it's time you started learnin'. Now you ain't crazy, for our folks don't go crazy, and you are goin' to register, and you are goin' to fight, and fight your darnedest, too, if your country calls you. Now just put that in your head and let it stay there. I don't want to hurt you, and I ain't if you do right; but I just want to say that if you don't do right, when I get you back home I will take you into the public square and shoot you myself in the presence of all the folks."

The boy, with tears in his eyes, said he would register just as quickly as he could.

"And I'll fight, too, if they want me," the boy added.

"Of course you will, for if you didn't you wouldn't be my son," the old man replied.

And that was the end of the Allen incident.

"That old fellow is one of the kind that makes the country great. He is a real American," said Judge Mayer afterward.

Just before he left the Federal Building, John Allen asked one of the deputy marshals what case was being tried before Judge Mayer. (It was the case of Emma Goldman and Alexander Berkman.)

"I noticed a man and a woman and I wondered who they were. What did they do?" he asked.

"They are anarchists and they are on trial for urging men not to register for the war," the Marshal replied.

"Those are the kind'er folks who are responsible for boys like this one of mine gettin' in trouble," John Allen observed. "We don't have folks like that down our way."

CONSOLING INFORMATION

Mrs. S. Kensington—"We have such good news from the front! Dear Charles is safely wounded, at last!"

HE WAS ALL RIGHT

Doctor—"Why were you rejected?"

Applicant (smiling)—"For imbecility."

"What do you do for a living?"

"Nothing; I have an income of six thousand dollars."

"Are you married?"

"Yes."

"What does you wife do?"

"Nothing; she is richer than I."

"You are no imbecile. Passed for general service."

THE 100-POUND TERROR OF THE AIR

WHEN he registered at a New York hotel the clerk looked him over with a supercilious eye. He was a trifle undersized, to be sure, and youngish—twenty-two and weighing only one hundred pounds. And the name, W. A. Bishop, hastily scrawled on the register, meant nothing to the clerk—probably some college stripling in town to give Broadway the once-over. But a little later the same clerk looked at that name on the hotel roster with a sensation as nearly approaching awe as a New York hotel clerk is capable of feeling; for he had learned that the diminutive guest was the world-famous Maj. William Avery Bishop, of the British Royal Flying Corps, who in three months won every decoration Great Britain has created to pin upon the breasts of her gallant fighters.

Mars is a grim god and an exacting master, but he sometimes "smoothes his wrinkled front" at the blandishments of the little god of Love. And it was so in the case of Major Bishop when the gallant knight of the air checked the war-god in the hotel coat room and slipped away with Dan Cupid to Toronto, where his sweetheart was waiting to welcome him. They are to be married before he returns to the front.

The St. Louis *Post-Dispatch* reckons Bishop as the greatest air fighter since Guynemer. It says of his exploits:

So far as is known, Major Bishop is the only living man who has a right to wear not only the Military Medal but the Order of Distinguished Service, and not only that, but the Victoria Cross. Yet he is only twenty-two years old, and he blushed and stammered like a schoolboy when he tried to explain something about air fighting at a Canadian club dinner in New York. However, here is his record as piled up in five months at the front:

One hundred and ten single combats with German fliers.

Forty-seven Hun airplanes sent crashing to the earth.

Twenty-three other planes sent down, but under conditions which made it impossible to know certainly that they and their pilots had been destroyed.

Thrilling escapes without number, including one fall of 4,000 feet with his machine in flames.

The most daredevil feat of the war—an attack single-handed on a *Boche* airdrome, in which he destroyed three enemy machines.

These feats not only won medals for the hero, but rapid promotion. With his appointment as Major, he was also named chief instructor of aerial gunnery—which is his chief hobby—and commander of an airplane squadron.

Bishop went to Europe from his home in Owen Sound, a little Ontario town, where his father is County Registrar, in the spring of 1915 as a cavalry private. Cavalrymen have an easy time these days waiting for the trench warfare to end and the coming of the open fighting, when they can get at the Hun. Bishop didn't want to wait, so he was transferred to the flying corps. He made no particular impression on these officers, but finally got a place as observer in the spring of 1916. His machine was shot down presently, and when he came out of hospital he was given three months' leave, most of which he spent at home.

When he went back last fall he tried again, and this time succeeded in qualifying as a pilot. He spent the early winter training in England, and finally reached the front in February. Then things began to happen.

His first enemy plane was brought down within a few days, under circumstances which have not been told, but which were enough to win the Military Medal. By Easter his record was such that he was made flight commander and captain. He celebrated by attacking three German planes single-handed. Four others came to their rescue. He got two; then out of ammunition, he went home. This brought him the D. S. O.

Bishop won the Victoria Cross in a sensational air battle. Here is the official account as given in *The Post-Dispatch:*

"Captain Bishop flew first to an enemy airdrome. Finding no enemy machine about, he flew to another about three miles distant and about twelve miles within enemy lines. Seven machines, some with their engines running, were on the ground. He attacked these from a height of fifty feet, killing one of the mechanics.

"One of the machines got off the ground, but Captain Bishop, at a height of sixty feet, fired fifteen rounds into it at close range. A second machine got off the ground, into which he fired thirty rounds at 150 yards. It fell into a tree. Two more machines rose from the airdrome, one of which he engaged at a height of 1,000 feet, sending it crashing to the ground. He then emptied a whole drum of cartridges into the fourth hostile machine and flew back to the station.

"Four hostile scouts were 1,000 feet above him for a mile during his return journey, but they would not attack. His machine gun was badly shot about by machine gun fire from the ground."

Apparently the official reporter was not interested in the Captain's condition. The damaged machine gun accounts for his strategic retreat, which satisfies officialdom. On Bishop's behalf, it should be remembered that an aviator lives very close to his machine gun during a fracas—if he lives.

Anyhow, Bishop got the V. C. for this before-breakfast excursion. When he was given a furlough, a few weeks ago, it was suggested that he stop at Buckingham Palace on his way home. There a rather small man with a light beard and a crown pinned the three medals on the breast of the Canadian.

Major Bishop himself is inclined to complain a little at the tools with which he has to work. His faith in incendiary bullets has been shattered, for instance.

"You want to bring the Hun down in flames if you can," he explained. "That is the nicest way. But you can't be sure of doing that. I shot six incendiary bullets into one fellow's petrol tank one day, and the thing wouldn't blow up."

Good shooting is what does the trick, he says, and plenty of it.

"Don't trust to one bullet to kill a Hun. Get him in the head if you can, or at least in the upper part of the body. But get him several times—one bullet is never sure to kill one. Get hunks of them into him; into his head. That does it. The greatest thing to teach the new man is how to shoot."

Sounds rather bloodthirsty, but this 100-pound fighter knows his enemy and of what he is capable. While Bishop finds bombing quite interesting, he prefers dueling, which he says is still seeking higher altitudes; in fact, when one is flying above 22,000 feet he is never sure that he will not be attacked from above. The unexpected appeals to Bishop, who cites the following as an enjoyable occasion:

"I was about 10,000 feet up, going through a cloud bank, without a thing in my mind but to get back six or seven miles behind the Hun lines and see what was going on, when I heard the rattle of machine guns. I looked back and there were three Huns coming straight for me. We all started firing at about 300 yards. I gave all I had to one fellow and he came to within about ten yards of me before swerving. He went by in flames. I turned on the second and he fell, landing only about 100 yards from the first one, which shows how fast we were going.

"I was excited, and the third machine escaped," he added apologetically.

An attack, two duels, and two victories while the planes were traveling less than a quarter of a mile, at over 100 miles an hour! Time, perhaps ten seconds.

It was Bishop, according to reports, who invented the plan of diving down and shooting the Germans from behind during an attack. He did not discuss the origin of the idea, but denied that it did much damage. Oh, yes, an occasional machine gun nest, but, then, there are only a few men in these. The real effect was moral. It distracts the Hun to be shot in the back. Also it greatly encourages the infantry who are charging.

"They cheer like mad," he grinned. "They think we are killing thousands of Huns."

Traditions gather thick around such a man. Tommy has no demigods in his religion, but he does the best he can with his heroes. So Tommy says that Bishop brought down nine machines in a two-hour fight one day. But Tommy's best story of him is given to illustrate the nerve which enjoys being called on to fight for life on a split second's notice.

A Hun flier had used an incendiary bullet on Bishop's petrol tank that did work, Tommy reports. The battle had been at a low altitude, about two miles up. Bishop's plane flamed up, and he fell. He was on the point of jumping and had loosed the straps that held him into the fuselage. Airmen dislike being burned to death. But he decided to make a try for life at the risk of this, and after he had fallen 4,000 feet or so took the levers again and pulled up the nose of the plane, straightening her out. Of course, his engine was out, so he began to tail dive, and went a few more thousand feet that way. Then he succeeded in straightening her out once more, but side-slipped, and finally banked just as he struck. One wing of his flaming machine hit first and broke the fall. The loosened straps let him jump clear. He was just behind the British lines, and Tommy rushed up and gathered him in and extinguished the fire in his blazing clothing.

He was not hurt.

THE WATCH-DOGS OF THE TRENCHES

THERE are stories a-plenty of the dash and fire of youth in the trenches. But by no means are all the men young who are battling on the front in France. There are the territorials, the line defenders, the men of the provinces, with wives and children at home.

"They are wonderful, these older fellows," said an officer enthusiastically, after a visit to the trenches. "They ought to be decorated—every one of them!"

It is of these watch-dogs of the trenches that René Bazin has written in *Lisez-Moi*, and the article, translated by Mary L. Stevenson, is printed in the Chicago *Tribune*. Mr. Bazin says:

I am proud of the young fighters, but those I am proudest of are the older ones. These have passed the age when the hot blood coursing through their veins drives them to adventure; they are leaving behind wife, children, present responsibilities, and future plans—those things hardest to cast off. Leaving all this, as they have done, without a moment's hesitation, is proof enough of their courage. And from the beginning of the war to the present time I have never talked to a solitary commanding officer that he has not eulogized his territorials.

They are essentially trench defenders, lookout men. The young ones do the coursing. These attack, the others guard. But how they do guard, how they hold the ground, once won! Nearing the front, if you meet them on the march as they are about to be relieved, you can recognize them even from afar by two signs: they march without any military coquetry, even dragging their feet a little, and they have everything with them that they can possibly carry—sacks, blankets, cans, bagpipes, cartridge-boxes, with the neck of a bottle sticking out of their trousers pocket. Even when you get near enough to see their faces many of these men do not look at you; they are intent upon their own thoughts. They know the hard week ahead of them. But the wind and rain are already old friends; the mud of the trenches does not frighten them; patience has long been their lot; they accept death's lottery, knowing well that they are protecting those they have left behind, and they go at it as to a great task whose harvest may not be reaped or even known until months later.

In truth, these men from the provinces—vine-growers, teamsters, little peasant farmers, the most numerous of all among today's combatants—will have played a magnificent rôle in the Great War. History will have to proclaim this, in justice to the French villages, and may the Government see fit to honor and aid these silent heroes who will have done so much to save the country.

They disappear quickly, lost in the defiles or swallowed up by the mist, which night has thickened. Once in the trenches, they find the work begun the previous week and which has been carried on by their comrades' hands, and when it comes their turn to guard the battlements they hide themselves in the same holes in the clay wall. No unnecessary movements, no flurry, no bravados, no setting off of flashes or grenade and bomb-throwing, by which the younger troops immediately show their presence in the trenches, and which only provokes a reply from the enemy.

They are holding fast, but they keep still about it. Suddenly the *Boches* are coming. There are some splendid sharpshooters in this regiment, and in the attack of the Seventh and in the surprise attempt of the Fourteenth at daybreak it was seen what these men could do. An officer said to me: "They suffer the least loss; they excel in shelters of earthwork, they merge right into the turf."

Many of the sectors of the front are held by this guard of older men. When the German reserves were hurled in pursuit of the Belgian Army in 1914, threatening the shores of Pas de Calais, a territorial division checked the onslaught of the best troops of the German Empire. Of their work in the trenches, Mr. Bazin writes:

But do not let anyone think theirs is a life of inaction; work is not lacking; even night is a time of reports, of revictualing, of reconnoitering, or repairing barbed-wire entanglements.

When the sector is quiet, however, the territorial enjoys some free hours. He writes a great deal; makes up for all the time past when he wrote almost no letters at all and for all the time to come when he promises himself to leave the pen hidden on the groove of the ink-well, idle on the mantel. One of them said to me: "They have put up a letter-box in my village. What will it be good for after the war—a swallow's nest?"

Many of these letters contain only a recital of uneventful days and the prescribed formalities of friendship or love, banal to the general public but dear enough to those who are waiting and who will sit around the lamp of an evening and comment on every word. I know young women throughout the country who receive a letter from their husbands every day. The war has served as a school for adults. Sometimes expediency entirely disappears and it is the race which speaks, and the hidden faith, and the soul which perhaps has never thus been laid bare.

Here is a letter which has been brought to my notice. For a year it had been carried in the pocket of a territorial who wrote it as his last will and testament, and when he was killed it was sent to his widow. Read it and see if you would not like to have had him who wrote it as a friend and neighbor:

"My dear, today, as I am writing these lines, my heart feels very big, and if you ever read them it will be because I died doing my duty. I ask you, before I go, to bring up our children in honor and in memory of me, for I have loved them very dearly, and I shall have died thinking of them and of you. Tell them I died on the field of honor, and that I ask them to offer the same sacrifice the day France shall need their arms and hearts. Preserve my certificate of good conduct, and later make them know that their father would like to have lived for them and for you, whom I have always held so dear. Now, I do not want you to pass the rest of your life worshiping one dead. On the contrary, if during your life you meet some good, industrious young fellow capable of giving you loyal aid in rearing our children, join your life with his and never speak to him of me, for if he loves you it would only cast the shadow of a dead man upon him—it is over, my dear. I love you now and forever, even through eternity. Good-bye! I shall await you over there. Your adoring Jean."

As showing the dogged, determined character of these men, Mr. Bazin relates the following incident:

Lately, when both wind and rain were raging, an officer told me of going up to two lookout men, immovable at their posts in the first line trench, and joking with them, he said:

"Let's see, what do you need?"

"Less mud."

"I am in the same boat. What else?"

"This and that—"

"You shall have it, I promise you. Tired?"

"A little."

"Discouraged?"

They made a terrible face, looked at him, and together replied: "If you have come to say such things as that, sir, you better not have come at all. Discouraged? No, indeed! We're not the kind who get discouraged!"

ALL IN THE SAME COUNTRY

The German officer who confiscated a map of Cripple Creek belonging to an American traveler, and remarked that "the German Army might get there some time," should be classed with the London banker who said to a solicitous mother seeking to send cash to San Antonio, Texas, for her wandering son: "We haven't any correspondent in San Antonio, but I'll give you a draft on New York, and he can ride in and cash it any fine afternoon."

GENERAL BELL REDEEMS HIS PROMISE

THE youngsters at Camp Upton looked with admiring and envious eyes at the ribbons pinned on the left breast of the man who entered headquarters. Then they looked up at the face of the wearer of these emblems of service in the Indian Wars, Cuba, and the Philippines, and they saw a sturdy campaigner of field and desert, his face bronzed by many scorching suns. On the left sleeve of his coat were the three bars of a sergeant with the emblem of the supply department in the inverted V.

This ghost of the old Army seemed to feel a little out of place for a moment, and then he turned to Sergeant Dunbaugh and said:

"I'd like to see the General, if you please."

"Have you an appointment?" asked Dunbaugh a bit hesitatingly.

"Well, no, but the General told me to come back, so I am here."

As the General was then out in the camp Sergeant Dunbaugh suggested that the old soldier tell him just what he wanted to see him about, and, says the New York *Sun:*

So the story of Sergeant Busick was told—the story of a once trim young trooper and a once dashing lieutenant of the Seventh Cavalry, immortalized by Custer and honored by a whole army.

Twenty years ago Edward Busick was assigned as a private to G Troop of the Seventh, stationed at Fort Apache, Arizona. At that time G was officially lacking a captain, so a certain young lieutenant was acting commander, and for his orderly he chose one Trooper Busick.

One evening, a year later, the lieutenant received sudden orders to report immediately to a staff post. All that night his orderly worked with him packing his personal belongings and helping him get ready for an early-morning start. It was a long job, and a hard one, but the orderly didn't mind the work in the least; all he cared about was the loss of his troop commander.

"Don't suppose I'll ever see you again, Busick, but if I do, and there's anything I can do for you, I'll be glad to do it," the lieutenant told him when the job was finished and the last box had been nailed down.

It wasn't very much for a lieutenant to say to his orderly, but it meant a great deal to this trim young trooper. Somehow, in the old Army, orderlies get to thinking a great deal of their officers and Busick happened to be just that particular kind. He had an especially good memory, too.

The whirligig of fate that seems to have so much to do with Army affairs sent the lieutenant to the Philippines, where, as colonel of the suicide regiment, he won everlasting honor for his regiment and a Congressional medal for valor for himself. Then on up he jumped until his shoulder-straps bore the single star of a brigadier. Then another star was added, and he became chief of staff and ranking officer in the whole Army.

And all the while the whirligig that looks after enlisted men saw to it that Trooper Busick added other colored bars to his service ribbons. And slowly he added pounds to his slim girth and a wife and children to his fireside. But as a heavy girth and a family aren't exactly synonymous with dashing cavalrymen, Sergeant Busick saw to it that he was transferred from the roving cavalry to the stationary Coast Artillery. And through all the years he remembered the lieutenant and his promise that if he ever wanted anything he would try to get it for him.

One month ago Sergeant Busick got a furlough from his Coast Artillery company at Fort McKinley, Portland, Me., and bought a ticket to Camp Upton, New York. There were only a few men here then, so he didn't have any great difficulty in seeing his old first lieutenant.

For half a minute or so General Bell, commanding officer of the Seventy-seventh Division of the National Army and one-time first lieutenant of the Seventh Cavalry, didn't recognize his old orderly—but it was for only half a minute.

"You'll sleep in our quarters with us tonight," General Bell ordered. "Tomorrow we'll see about that old promise."

So that night Sergeant Busick had the room between Major-General Bell's and Brigadier-General Read's. But sleeping next to generals was pretty strong for an ordinary sergeant and he didn't accept General Bell's invitation to have mess with him.

And a little later Busick told his old commander that the big request that he had come across the continent to make was that he be transferred to the Seventy-seventh division and allowed to serve under the General. But army tape is still long and red, so all that the General could do was to send the sergeant back to his post and promise that he would do all that he could. This, it proved, was sufficient.

For Sergeant Edward Busick, smiling and happy with his reassignment papers safely tucked away in the pocket of his blouse under his half a foot of service ribbons, came back to report for duty. It took twenty years to do—but he's done it.

And the National Army of Freedom hasn't any idea as yet how much richer in real soldier talent and color it is today. But a certain old campaigner, who used to be a first lieutenant of cavalry, knows.

NO GREAT LOSS

An American stopping at a London hotel rang several times for attendance, but no one answered. He started for the office in an angry mood, which was not improved when he found that the "lift" was not running. Descending two flights of stairs, he met one of the chambermaids.

"What's the matter with this dashed hotel?" he growled. "No one to answer your call and no elevator running."

"Well, you see, sir," said the maid, "the Zeps were reported and we were all ordered to the cellar for safety."

"——!" ejaculated the American. "I was on the fifth floor and I wasn't warned."

"No, sir," was the bland reply, "but you see, sir, you don't come under the Employers' Liability Act, sir."

LETTERS FROM THE FRONT

"LAST evening we went out into a field, and read Jane Austen's 'Emma' out loud."

Do you get the picture? Can you see the fading glory of the sunset sky, and hear the soft breeze, sweetly laden with the scent of new-mown hay, as it murmurs through the gently rustling leaves—a real autumn scene of rural peace and quiet?

Yes? Well, you are quite mistaken. That is an extract from a letter written by an ambulance driver on the French front. And so you see that war is not all horror.

Emerson Low, the son of Alfred M. Low, of Detroit, went to France with a group of college boys. He joined the American Field Ambulance Service, and is now in the thick of the fighting in the Champagne district. The Detroit *Free Press* prints some extracts from his letters to his family. In one he tells of his trip to the posts:

Day before yesterday several of us started out for the posts. I carried the *médecin divisionnaire* and went a little before the others. In spite of the fact that the fields are being recultivated and the searness of former battles is somewhat concealed, the road to the front is rather a grim affair, and you are startled when you pass through a town deserted and demolished. There is quite a large town between this one and the front. It is uninhabited except for a few soldiers and a yellow dog that slinks about in the doorways.

I left the *médecin divisionnaire* at his *abri*, a little further along the road, a road hidden completely by strips of burlap tied to poles. The first post is in a little wood. There were two of us there, and we tossed a coin to see who would take the first call. I won and waited for an ambulance to come in from one of our three posts. These posts are along the front of the hill where the battle is taking place. They are all reached by going through and then beyond X (you remember the little destroyed town with the church which I spoke of during our first month). The first post was a smaller town than X, and is now razed completely to the ground. The second is about one-fourth of a mile to the right and the third—which can only be reached during the night and left before dawn—is a German *abri*, formerly a dugout of German officers. The German *saucises* are directly above the road, and any machine would be shelled in the daytime. The posts are close together and are reached by exposed roads.

My call came about noon. I was given an orderly, and left for the first post. From the road we could see the shells breaking on the hill and in the fields about, where the French batteries were hidden. We reached the post, backed the machine into a wide trench, which hid it from view, and then went into the dugout. It was a new iron dugout, about 30 feet long and 10 or 12 feet broad, with bunks on either side. On top were heaped bags of sand and dirt.

We read until about two o'clock, when several shells fell in the battery field a few meters behind us. Then a few shells fell in a field to the right, and in another moment we were in the midst of a bombardment. It lasted all afternoon. Two men trying to enter the dugout were hit, one in the throat and the other in the shoulder, but not badly. About six o'clock it grew so bad and so many shells fell on the roof of the dugout that we had to leave, cross through some trenches—a strange-looking procession, crouching and running along—and get into a deep cave about twenty feet under the ground, where we stayed until eight o'clock in the evening. Then the firing became intermittent, the shells hit further to the right and left, and we ran back into the dugout.

It was still light and an airplane soared above us, the noise of which is to me, for an unaccountable reason, one of the most reassuring sounds I have ever heard.

Quite jocularly he writes of supper, first having looked at his car which he found uninjured, although covered with dirt from exploding shells. Continuing, he says:

There were about eight of us, the orderly and myself, the lieutenant-doctor in charge, and three or four old *brancardiers*, who, when they ate their soup made more noise than the shells. After every few spoonfuls, to avoid waste, they poked their mustaches in their mouths and sucked them loudly.

During the evening the firing became steady on both sides, the French battery pouring their shells, which whistled over our dugout. We went to bed, secure in this iron cylinder, whose great ribs stood like the fleshless carcass of a beast, which to destroy would be a worthless task. A stump of a candle lay wrapped in our blankets in the bunks. It was rather comfortable, except that my bed was crossed at the top by a piece of iron just where my head lay.

All through the night there was a continuous commotion in the dugout, the *brancardiers* running around and talking in loud voices about things we were too sleepy to understand. We had no *blessés* during the night (an exceptional thing—this morning they had fifty from one post) and were relieved about half-past ten the next morning. I returned to the large town, where our cantonment had been changed to another quarter of the village.

This is an exceptionally fine cantonment and was recently occupied by the British Ambulance, whose place we have taken. I think it was originally an officers' barracks. Two low cement buildings, faced with red brick and roofed with red tile, stand on one side, and opposite these are the stables, used by the "Genies." In front of the houses are some trees and grass. Each house (one story in height) is divided into four parts, accessible by four doors.

Jim, Rogers, and I have one room to ourselves off the third hallway and in front. There are three other rooms accessible by the same hallway. It is almost like a separate house, as each division has its flight of steps before the door and there is a main sidewalk running under all the front windows. We have our three stretchers on the floor, two cupboards, a broken mirror, and two camp-stools. We keep our trunks, etc., right in the room and it saves transferring them every trip to the posts. There is a large French window with blue shutters. We certainly are comfortably located. There are no showers after all (we had expected two), except one that is broken, and we wash from our *bidons* (canteens) with a sponge, which is almost as good.

Jim and Rogers came back yesterday shortly before I did. They had both been to the same post, the second one, and been caught in a gas-attack which lasted for an hour. They sat in the *abri* with their masks on (the masks are a greenish color, with two big round windows for the eyes) and, of course, with the helmets, the *abri* was crowded, and from their description they must have looked like so many big beetles crouching together. There is absolutely no danger with the masks, however, and we carry one always with us (even in town) and one fastened in the car.

Last evening we went out into a field and read Jane Austen's "Emma" out loud. Jim and Rog left this morning for the posts and I go tomorrow.

Of the routine work of the ambulance driver he writes:

On account of the night driving we have lately put two men on each car, a driver and an orderly who just goes back and forth between the posts. Five cars are out every day and eight drivers. Three cars begin at the posts and two wait in the woods. As a car comes in from a post, another is sent out from the woods and this driver takes with him the orderly who has just come in, as only one man is necessary to make the trip from the woods to the hospital. From the hospital the latter returns to the woods, and thus a relay is formed. The day before yesterday I was at post 1; yesterday (beginning at noon), I was *en repos* for the day; today I am *en remplacement*, that is practically the same as repose, but if any extra cars are wanted in case of an attack, etc., we have to be within call. I am fourth in the list and don't expect to go out. Tomorrow I go in my own car, next day repose, next day as orderly to post 3, next day repose, etc. The work is as interesting as ever.

In another letter which *The Free Press* prints Mr. Low tells of a battle between airplanes directly over his head. The engagement ended with the winging of both machines. The letter reads:

The German machine fell between the lines, the French plane near one of our posts. There was a terrific fight, which we could hardly see, as it was very high in the air. The French plane caught on fire and began to fall. After some meters it was entirely enveloped in smoke and the three aviators had to jump, which was a quicker death. When they were found, parts of their bodies had been burned away.

Just before this the first German shell fell in our cantonment. It was about half-past seven in the morning and we were all asleep when we heard the rush and explosion of an *obus*. It struck about two meters from the barracks and made a large hole in the road. Three shells usually fall in one place, but no other followed.

For a day of repose it certainly was disturbing.

Yesterday I had a hot shower at the hospital near here. It certainly seemed good, after bathing for two months out of a small reserve water can.

This morning we are at the second post. Before the war there were really enough houses to call it a small town, but it has been so completely destroyed that only stumps of the buildings remain. Batteries have been planted all about it, and at present they are receiving a heavy shelling from the Germans.

Mr. Low seems to possess an excellent nervous organization and a dependable imagination which he finds quite useful. He says:

We are kept in the dugout, which, provided with chairs and a table, is very comfortable. It is rather pleasant to be securely seated here with books and listening to the "rush" of the shells overhead. It is like being before a grate fire and listening to a winter's storm outside. As long as no *blessés* are brought in we can sit here and warm our feet until the storm is over. Our beds are all made on the stretchers (placed high enough to keep out the rats), and we intend to spend a pleasant afternoon reading. I have Rog's Shakespeare, and I am reading "Cymbeline."

We have just had lunch—hot meat, lentils, camembert, and the inevitable Pinard. The bombardment has nearly died away, so we can sit out a while and enjoy a very delightful August day. This post is reached by an old Roman road, which is rather badly torn up. They have just put up a screen of burlap to conceal it from the *saucisses;* that is, to hide the traffic on it, for the German gunners know where every road lies.

(Later) A young fellow of about nineteen was just carried in. He was at the battery post a few meters behind us and became half-crazed by the shells during the bombardment. It is quite a common occurrence, especially with the men in the trenches. The French call it *commotion,* and the mind becomes so stunned that often they lose their speech or become totally stupid. The lieutenant said that this was a bad case and that if another shell fell near the man he would go mad. He asked us to take the fellow back to the hospital as soon as possible, and I had to ride in the back of the ambulance with him all the way to keep him quiet. Fortunately no shells came near the car.

After supper we sat near the edge of the road and watched two or three battalions pass by on their way to the trenches. The road filled with carts and supply wagons as soon as the *saucisses* descended. These vehicles travel between towns in the rear to a communication trench a little beyond our post, a point which is a terminus for all traffic. From there the ammunition and supplies are carried to the trenches by hand.

There is a little railroad running from that point, beyond our post; horses pulling small flat cars loaded with wood, barbed wire, etc., for the trenches. A young *poilu,* standing up and waving his arms, came spinning down the hill in an empty car. He nearly caused a collision and I never saw a man so yelled and screamed at as this one was by his sergeant.

The officer scolded him for a quarter of an hour and shouted himself hoarse: "*Quelle bêtise!*"

About nine we went down into the *abri*, lighted a candle on the table, and read until about ten, when a man burst through the door, shouting:

"*Gaz! Gaz! M. Médecin!*" and dashed out again. The *médecin* went outside, and, returning, told us to have our masks ready, that gas was coming over the hill and blowing in our direction. We waited about ten minutes and heard the alarm bell ring—a signal to warn that a gas attack is near. We sat waiting with our masks at our elbows, but the wind carried the gas in another direction and we did not have to use them.

These attacks are frequent, but not dangerous; as at every hour of the day a man stands in the first line trench (with a bell at his side) to give warning of gas. The masks that we always carry at our belts are positive guards against any sort of gas.

We read until twelve and then went to bed, lucky in having only one trip through the day.

HELPING HIS WIFE OUT

An officer was surprised one day when searching the letters of his detachment to read in one of them a passage that was something like this:

"We have just got out of shell-fire for the first time for two months. It has been a hard time. The Germans were determined to take our field bakery, but, by gee! we would not let them. We killed them in thousands."

This was a letter from one of the bakers to his wife. None of the detachment had been a mile from the base, and they had never seen a German, except as a prisoner. My friend knew the writer well, and could not help (although it was none of his business) asking him why he told such terrible lies to his poor wife. The soldier said:

"It's quite true what you say, but it's like this, sir. When my wife and the wives of the other men in the place where I live are talking it all over in the morning I couldn't think to let her have nothing to say and the others all bragging about what their men had done with the Germans. That's the way of it, sir."

MEET TOMMY, D. C. MEDAL MAN

IF war is not a great leveler—and we have been told numberless times that it is—it is certainly the Great American Mixer, and Camp Upton, L. I., is probably the best example extant thereof, so to speak. The Bowery boy and the millionaire rub elbows—you have probably heard that before, but it is nevertheless true—and the owners of Long Island show places sleep in cots next to their former gardeners. But probably the most interesting character at Camp Upton is the barber who was at one time a sergeant in the British Flying Corps, and wears the King's Distinguished Conduct Medal—that is, he probably would wear it if he hadn't left it at "'ome in a box." The New York *Sun* says:

Down on the muster pay roll the D. C. medal man is Harry Booton, but over in the 304th Field Artillery's headquarters company barracks they call him Ben Welch, the Jewish comedian. But for all that his real name is *Ortheris*, who even Kipling himself thought had lain dead these twenty years and more in the hill country of India. And for the brand of service for his reincarnation he has chosen the artillery—the bloomin', bloody artillery that he used to hate so much when he and *Mulvaney* were wearing the infantry uniform of the little old Widow of Windsor.

London cockney he was then, a quarter of a century ago, and London cockney he is today. And if there be some who say his name is not really *Ortheris*, let it be stated that names are of small moment after all. It's the heart that counts—and the heart of this under-sized little Jewish cockney is the heart of Kipling's hero—and the soul is his and the tale is his. And instead of telling his yarn to *Mulvaney* he now tells it to an Italian barber they call Eddie rather than his own gentle name of Gasualdi.

From Headquarters Hill, where the Old Man With the Two Stars looks out and down on his great melting-pot that's cooking up this stirring army of freedom, you walk a half mile or so west until you stumble on Rookie Roose J 18, where the headquarters company and the band of the 304th Field Artillery play and sing and sleep and work. In one corner of the low, black-walled washroom nestling next the big pine barracks, Eddie the Barber lathers, shaves, and clips hair for I. O. U.'s when he isn't busy soldiering. And into Eddie's ears come stories of girls back home and yarns of mighty drinking bouts of other days, and even tales of strange lands and wars and cabbages and kings. Eddie is the confidant of headquarters company.

If you stand around on one foot and then another long enough, and add a bit now and then to the gaiety of the nations represented in Eddie's home concocted tonsorial parlor you'll hear some of these wild yarns pass uninterrupted from the right to the left ear of Eddie. And if you're lucky you may even hear the tale of the D. C. medal—and the five wounds, and the torpedoed bark, and the time the King's hand was kissed, and all from the lips of *Ortheris*, alias Harry C. Booton, alias Ben Welch.

And so, if you will kindly make way for the hero, whose medal is "at 'ome in me box,"—but who did not forget to bring his cockney accent along, to which he has added a dash of the Bowery—you may listen to the tale that was told to the *Sun* man:

"I was boined down in Whitechapel, Lunnon, and me ole man died seventeen years ago in the Boer War," the tongue of Harry began his tale: "'E was a soger under 'Mackey' McKenzie, and 'e was kilt over in Sout Africey. Well, when Hingland goes into this war I says to meself I'll join out to an' do me bit, an' so I done wit' the Lunnon Fusileers, and after two or three months trainin' we was sint to Anthwerp, but we didn't stop there very long.

"Then we fights in the battle of Mons and Lille—I don't know how you spells that Lille, but I think it's 'L-i-l'—or somethin' loik that. Well, in the battle of Mons I gets blowed up. Funny about that. You see, a Jack Johnson comes along and buries me, all except me bloomin' feet, and then I gets plugged through both legs with a rifle bullet and I'm in the hospital for a month. When I gets out I'm transferred to the Royal Flying Corps and I goes to the Hendon or sumthin' loike that aereodrome up Mill Hill way, fur trainin'. You see, I was a stige electrician in the Yiddish teaters on the Edgware road, and knowin' things like that I was mide a helper and learnt all about flying machines."

The b-r-r-r-r of an airplane—the first one to fly over the camp—caused Henry's ear to cock for a second and then a smile to pop out of his face.

"'Ere's one of the bloomin' things now," he went on. "Well, I was made a sergeant an' arfter a bad bomin' of Lunnon by the Fritzes six of us machines was sent to pay compliments to the Germans.

"It was dark and cold and nasty when we started out to attack Frederickshaven and give 'em some of their own medicine.

"Three hundred miles we flies an' I'd dropped eighteen of my nineteen bums—you see I was riding with Sergeant-Major Flemming—when they opens up on us with their antiguns and five of us flops down, blazin' and tumblin'. Then somethin' hits me back and somethin' else stings me arm and then I felt her wabble and flop. I glances behind and my sergeant is half fallin' out and just as he tumbled I mikes a grab for 'im. 'E was right behint me and so as to right the machine I grips him with me teeth in his leather breetches and then I throws 'im back and swings into his seat and tramps on the pedal for rising. Up we goes to 9,000 feet, but it was too bloomin' cold up there, so I come down some and points back for Hingland.

"The sergeant 'e were there with me, and I was glad efen if 'e had been kilt dead. You wouldn't want 'im back there with them *Booches*—'im my pal and my sergeant. I wasn't going to let the *Booches* have 'im.

"More'n 300 miles I had to fly—6 degrees it were—when I caught Queensborough, and then I come down. Funny about that—just as soon as I 'it the ground I fainted loike a bloomin' lidy.

"An' I was up in a Hinglish 'ospital in Lunnon when I come to a couple of d'ys after. An' I wykes a bloomin' 'ero, and the King 'e sends for me an' some other 'eroes, and we all goes to Buckingham Palace, and 'is Majesty the King and Queen Mary and a ole bloomin' mess of them bloomin' dooks and lydies comes and the King pins the medal on me. Me a 'ero with a D. C. medal. And now I'm warin' this bloomin' kiki-ki and hopin' to get another crack at Kaiser Bill and Fritz the sauerkraut."

The 'ero was finally invalided out of service and ordered to the munitions factories in northern England. Having no inclination for this work, he stowed away on the Swedish bark *Arendale*, which was torpedoed when fifteen days out from London. He was picked up by the Dutch steamship *Leander* and finally landed in New Orleans. The *Sun* continues:

Then Harry came to New York a little over a year ago and made his abode at 157 Rivington street. By day he worked in a A-Z Motion Picture Supply Company, 72 Hester street, and by night he told brave tales of war and sang snatches of opera that he had learned behind the scenes in London.

Then came America's entrance into the Great War and the selective service examination. At Board 109 Harry demanded that although he was a British subject he be allowed to go. And after considerable scratching of heads the members of Board 109 decided to ship Harry to Camp Upton with the first increment on September 10, and what was more, to make him the squad leader on the trip.

"Salute me, ya bloomin' woodchopper," Harry, ex-Tommy Atkins, shouted in derision at some lowly private who ventured to try a light remark. "Hain't I yer superior? Hain't I actin' corporal? Hain't I goin' to be a sergeant-major? Awsk me—hain't I?"

And the answer was decidedly and emphatically yes. And power to ye, Harry Booton—medal or no medal.

GERMAN FALCON KILLED IN AIR-DUEL

THE old days when armies ceased fighting to watch their two champions in single combat have come back again. It was on the Western front, and the engagement that resulted in the death of Immelman the Falcon, Germany's most distinguished Ace, was in very truth a duel—no chance meeting of men determined to slay one another, but a formally arranged encounter, following a regular challenge, and fought by prearrangement and without interference. The battle was witnessed with breathless interest by the men of both armies crouched in the trenches, separated by only a few feet of No Man's Land, while the fire of the anti-aircraft guns on both sides was stilled.

The victor in the spectacular fight was Captain Ball, the youthful English pilot who has only two notches less on the frame of his fighting machine than had the Falcon, who was credited with fifty-one "downs." The story of the duel, which was declared to have been one of the most sensational events of the war, is told in a letter written by Col. William Macklin, of the Canadian troops, to a friend in Newark, N. J. Colonel Macklin, who was one of the eye-witnesses of the fight, writes in his letter, which is printed in the New York *Tribune:*

One morning Captain Ball, who was behind our sector, heard that Immelman the Falcon was opposite.

"This is the chance I've been waiting for; I'm going to get him," declared Ball.

Friends tried to dissuade him, saying the story of Immelman's presence probably was untrue. Ball would not listen.

Getting into his machine, he flew over the German lines and dropped a note which read:

"Captain Immelman: I challenge you to a man-to-man fight, to take place this afternoon at two o'clock. I will meet you over the German lines. Have your anti-aircraft guns withhold their fire while we decide which is the better man. The British guns will be silent.

"Ball."

About an hour afterward, a German aviator swung out across our lines. Immelman's answer came. Translated it read:

"Captain Ball: Your challenge is accepted. The German guns will not interfere. I will meet you promptly at two.

"Immelman."

Just a few minutes before two o'clock the guns on both sides ceased firing. It was as though the commanding officers had ordered a truce. Long rows of heads popped up and all eyes watched Ball from behind the British lines shoot off and into the air. A minute or two later Immelman's machine was seen across No Man's Land.

The letter describes the tail of the German machine as painted red "to represent the British and French blood it had spilled," while Ball's had a streak of black paint to represent the mourning for his victims. The machines ascended in a wide circle, and then:

From our trenches there were wild cheers for Ball. The Germans yelled just as vigorously for Immelman.

The cheers from the trenches continued. The Germans' increased in volume; ours changed into cries of alarm.

Ball, thousands of feet above us and only a speck in the sky, was doing the craziest things imaginable. He was below Immelman and was, apparently, making no effort to get above him, thus gaining the advantage of position. Rather he was swinging around, this way and that, attempting, it seemed, to postpone the inevitable.

We saw the German's machine dip over preparatory to starting the nose dive.

"He's gone now," sobbed a young soldier at my side, for he knew Immelman's gun would start its raking fire once it was being driven straight down.

Then, in the fraction of a second, the tables were turned. Before Immelman's plane could get into firing position, Ball drove his machine into a loop, getting above his adversary and cutting loose with his gun and smashing Immelman by a hail of bullets as he swept by.

Immelman's airplane burst into flames and dropped. Ball, from above, followed for a few hundred feet and then straightened out and raced for home. He settled down, rose again, hurried back, and released a huge wreath of flowers almost directly over the spot where Immelman's charred body was being lifted from a tangled mass of metal.

Four days later Ball, too, was killed. He attacked single-handed four Germans. He had shot one down and was pursuing the other three when two machines dropped from behind the clouds and closed in on him. He was pocketed and was killed—but not until he had shot down two more of the enemy.

HE TAUGHT THE "TANK" TO PROWL AND SLAY

ALONG with many other things with finer names, for which credit is due him, Col. E. D. Swinton, of the British Royal Engineers, will go down in history as the father of the tank, that modern war monster and engine of destruction which made its professional début on the Somme battlefield and which did such effective work in French and British drives.

Colonel Swinton is a pleasant, mild-mannered gentleman, the last person in the world one would expect to bear any relationship to the tank. In fact, the virtue of modesty in him is so well developed that he refuses to accept all the glory, and insists upon sharing the parental honors with an American, Benjamin Holt, inventor of the tractor.

"I don't mean that the Holt tractor is the tank by any means," he says, "but without the Holt tractor there very probably would not have been any tank."

Arthur D. Howden Smith, writing in the New York *Evening Post*, declares:

It is practically impossible to get Colonel Swinton to admit outright that he is the parent of the tank; yet father it he did, and he was also the first captain of the tanks in the British Army; he organized the tank unit in France, and he launched the loathly brood of his offspring in their initial victory on the Somme battlefield. If any man knows the tank, he does, for he created it and tamed it and taught it how to prowl and slay.

Colonel Swinton began to think about tanks several years before Austria sent her ultimatum to Servia, but he is scrupulously careful to say that many men were thinking more or less vaguely along the same lines at the same time. Indeed, the proposal of the tank as an engine for neutralizing the effect of machine gun fire was actually made by two sets of men, one to the War Office and one to the Admiralty, and neither group was aware that the other was working along the same lines. Still, we may believe unprejudiced testimony which gives to Colonel Swinton the principal credit for convincing the higher authorities in London that mobile land-forts were practicable.

"In July, 1914, I heard that Mr. Benjamin Holt, of Peoria, Ill., had invented a tractor which possessed the ability to make its way across rugged and uneven ground," he stated. "But several years before that a plan for a military engine practically identical with the tank had been sketched upon paper, when a tractor of another make was tried out in England. That first plan came to nothing. We weren't ready for it then.

"The reports of the Holt tractor served to stimulate my interest in the idea all over again, and when I went to France with Lord French in August, 1914, and saw what modern warfare was like, I became convinced that an armored car, capable of being independent of roads and of traversing any terrane to attack fortified positions, was a necessity for the offensive."

The Colonel, with a quizzical smile, here called attention to the fact that the principal German weapon of slaughter was the invention of an American—Hiram Maxim—and he thought it quite fitting that the weapon to combat it should be credited, at least in part, to the American inventor of the tractor. Continuing, he said:

"By October, 1914, I had a fair conception of the kind of engine which might be relied upon to neutralize the growing German power in machine guns, combined with the most elaborate fortifications ever built on a grand scale. You see, their fire ascendency in the meantime had enabled them to dig in with their usual thoroughness. In October I returned to England to try to interest the authorities at the War Office in my idea. I had my troubles, but I did not have as many troubles as I might have had, because other men of their own accord were working along the same lines.

"You must get this very straight, mind. Whatever credit there may be for inventing the tanks belongs not to any one man, but to many men—exactly how many nobody knows. It is even rather unfair to mention any names, my own as well as those of others. For, besides those men who actually worked to perfect the tanks, there were others who had conceived very similar ideas.

"Still another proof of the plurality of tank inventors is the fact that while one group of us were endeavoring to interest the War Office in the idea, another group of men, entirely ignorant of what we were doing, were trying to get the Admiralty to take up a similar line of experimentation. And it is no more than fair to point out that the first money provided for experimentation with landships, as we called them, came from Winston Spencer Churchill, then First Lord of the Admiralty. But he was only one of a number of men who played parts in the development of the finished engine. For example, there were two men in particular who worked out the mechanical problems. I wish I could give you their names, but I cannot."

To the suggestion of the writer in *The Post* that it seemed strange that so many minds should have been working out the same idea at the same time, Colonel Swinton replied emphatically:

"Not when you consider the situation. The tank, after all, is merely an elaboration, the last word, of military devices as old as the history of military engineering. Its ancestors were the armored automobile, the belfry or siege tower on wheels of the middle ages, and the Roman *testudo*. The need for the tank became apparent to many who studied the military problems demonstrated on the Western front. That is often so in the history of inventions, you know. A given problem occupies many minds simultaneously, and generally several reach a solution about the same time, even though perhaps one receives the credit for the invention above all the others."

"You spoke about the mechanical problems of the tanks. What were they?"

"Ah, there you are getting on delicate ground. I am glad to tell you all I can about the tanks, but I can't describe them—not beyond a certain point, that is. I will say just this—the peculiar original feature of them, upon which their efficiency most depends, is the construction of their trackage. It is the feature which enables them not only to negotiate rough and broken ground, but to surmount obstacles and knock down trees and houses. But the full description of the tanks cannot be written until after the war."

Colonel Swinton described the uproarious mirth of the British infantry on that morning when they had their first sight of the unwieldy tanks clambering over trenches, hills, small forests, and houses, spitting flames as they rolled, lolloping forward like huge armored monsters of the prehistoric past.

"It gave our men quite a moral lift," he said. "They forgot their troubles. But they soon came to see that the tanks were more than funny, for wherever they attacked the infantry had comparative immunity from machine gun fire, and it is the German machine gun fire which always has been the principal obstacle for our troops."

The name of the tank Colonel Swinton explained was originally a bit of *camouflage*. People who saw them in the process of erection variously described them as snowplows for the Russian front and water tanks for the armies in Egypt. The latter name stuck. And it may not be generally known that this mechanical beast of war is divided into two sexes.

"Some tanks are armed with small guns firing shells," said Colonel Swinton. "These are used especially against machine gun nests. They are popularly known in the tank unit as males. Other tanks carry machine guns and are intended primarily for use against enemy infantry. They are the females. There is no difference in the construction."

Colonel Swinton was detailed from his post in the British War Cabinet to act as assistant to Lord Reading in his mission to the United States to tighten the bonds of efficiency between the two countries in their war programs.

During the fall of 1914, Colonel Swinton was the English official eye-witness of the fighting in Flanders and France. Before that he was perhaps best known to the general public as a writer of romances in which was skillfully woven the technique of war. One of his stories, "The Defense of Duffer's Drift," is used as a text-book at West Point.

NOT A SELF-STARTER

"Sam, you ought to get in the aviation service," a Chicago man told a negro last week. "You are a good mechanic and would come in handy in an aeroplane. How would you like to fly among the clouds a mile high and drop a few bombs down on the Germans?"

"I ain't in no special hurry to fly, Cap," the negro answered. "When wese up 'bout a mile high, s'pose de engine stopped and de white man told me to git out an' crank?"

TRY IT ON YOUR WIFE

Extract from lecture by N. C. O.:

"Your rifle is your best friend, take every care of it; treat it as you would your wife; rub it thoroughly with an oily rag every day."

HE WAS GOING AWAY FROM THERE

He—"So your dear count was wounded?"
She—"Yes, but his picture doesn't show it."
He—"That's a front view."

TAKING MOVING PICTURES UNDER SHELL-FIRE

TAKING moving pictures while exploding shells from pursuing warships and torpedo-boats are sending up geysers that splash your fleeing launch and stall the motor is a little out of the run of even an American war correspondent's daily stunt. Capt. F. E.

Kleinschmidt, who has been billeted with the Austrian marine forces at Trieste, has recently had such an experience while accompanying an expedition to the Italian coast to remove a field of mines, an occupation quite dangerous enough without the shell-fire. He tells this story in the St. Louis *Post-Dispatch:*

Captain M——, commander of the marine forces of Trieste, had told me I should hold myself ready at a moment's notice for an interesting adventure. Presuming it would be another airplane flight over the enemy's territory, I kept my servants and chauffeur up late, and then finally lay down, fully dressed, with cameras and instruments carefully overhauled and packed. At seven o'clock next morning the boatswain of the launch *Lena* called at the hotel and told me to follow him. "The captain," he said, "could not accompany me." But he had instructions to take me out to sea and then obey my orders. An auto took us to the pier, where a fast little launch was ready. This time she had a machine gun, with ready belt attached, mounted in her stern, and flew the Austrian man-of-war flag. Not until we were well out to sea did the boatswain tell me we were to sneak over to the Italian shore and demolish a hostile mine field. The prevailing fog and exceptionally calm weather made it an ideal day to accomplish our purpose. The fog prevented the Italians from seeing us, and the calm sea made it possible to lift and handle the mines with a minimum of danger to ourselves. Two tugboats and a barge had already preceded us early in the morning. After an hour's run the three vessels suddenly appeared before us, and we drew alongside the tugboat No. 10, already busy hoisting a mine. I jumped aboard and reported to Captain K——, in charge of the expedition.

To my chagrin he refused to let me stay. The first reason was, it was too dangerous work, and he would not take the responsibility of my being blown up; and, secondly, we might be surprised by the Italians at any moment and be sent to the bottom of the sea. All my arguing and insisting upon the orders from his superior proved useless. He insisted upon my return or written orders clearing him of all responsibility. So I had to go back in the launch to Trieste and report to Captain M—— about the scruples of the commander of the mine expedition. I also offered to leave my servants (two Austrian soldiers) ashore and sign a written waiver of all responsibility should anything happen to me.

The ever-generous and obliging Captain M—— said he would accompany me himself, so out we raced for the second time, and I had the satisfaction to stay and photograph. The most dangerous work, namely, the lifting of the first mine, had been accomplished during my return to Trieste. The nature of the beast had been ascertained. The construction was a new one, of the defensive type. With good care and a smooth sea, the mines could be hoisted, made harmless and be saved. There would be, he hoped, no explosions, and, working quietly, we would not draw an Italian fleet down upon us.

There are mines of offensive and defensive purposes—such as you lay in front of your own harbors to protect you, and such as you lay in front of the doors of your enemy. The first ones you might want to move again; therefore, they are so constructed that you can handle them again, provided you know the secret of construction. The other kind you don't expect to touch again, and they are, therefore, so constructed that anyone who tampers with them will blow himself up. Secondly, should the Italians surprise us, there would be little chance for us to escape. We could steam only about ten knots an hour, while any cruiser or torpedo could steam over twenty. The only armament we had was one 75-millimeter Hotchkiss gun in the bow. There would be no surrender, either. He would blow the barge and his own steamer up first.

"Here," he said, pointing to a tin can the size of a tomato can, with ready short fuse attached, "is the bomb to be thrown in the barge, and here," looking down into the forward hold, "is the other one, ready to blow us into eternity. Now, if you want to stay, you're welcome; if not, take the launch back to Trieste."

Capt. M——, after a brief inspection, went back with the launch to Trieste, while I stayed and photographed with the moving picture camera.

There is a long international law governing the laying and exploding of mines, and there has been considerable controversy about the unlawful laying of anchored and drifting mines. There are land-, river-, and sea-mines. Mines laid for the protection of harbors are usually exploded by electric batteries from an observing officer on shore. Others are exploded by contact. The mechanical devices to accomplish this are manifold. The policy adhered to is usually to construct a mine so as to incur the least danger, when handling them, to yourself, and with the opposite results to your enemy. This holds true as long as the secret of construction can be kept from the enemy. The Italians on a night invasion had dropped mines on the Austrian coast that would explode when tilted only at an angle of twenty-five degrees. A little vial of acid would spill over and explode the charge. One day, when a heavy sea was running, some of the mines exploded, betraying the location of the mine field, and the Austrians "killed" the rest of them with minesweepers.

Mine fields are discovered by shallow-draft steamers looking for them in clear water or dragging for them. The aeroplane is also an excellent scout. From a height of 1,000 feet he can look a good depth into the sea and see a mine or submarine. On my flight over Grado, on the Italian coast, I could see a mine field and all shallows of a channel wonderfully well from a height of 6,000 feet. When the hydroplane sees a mine an automatic float is dropped that marks the locality, and the mines boat comes along and either lifts it or blows it up.

Here these Italian mines were of a late and very expensive construction. They consisted of three parts—the mine, the anchor, and a 100-pound weight; all three connected with a wire cable. The weight is an ordinary oval lump of iron, attached by a cable to the anchor. The anchor is a steel cylinder; the upper part is perforated; the lower half is a tank with a hole in the bottom and sides to allow the water to enter and sink it. The mine is a globe two and one-half feet in diameter, which fits into the barrel-like anchor up to its equator.

The weight, cable, and anchor holding the mine are rolled from the mine-laying ship, overboard. The weight sinks to the bottom, holding the mine in the spot. Next, the water entering the tank slowly fills it, and it sinks at the designated place. The mine, being buoyant, has detached itself from the sinking anchor and is pulled down with the anchor and floats now at a depth of eight to twelve feet from the surface. The water now dissolves a peculiar kind of cement that has held a number of pistons. The pistons, being released, spring out and snap in place all around the equator of the mine. Comes a vessel in contact with the mine, these protruding points, made of brittle metal, break off and a spring releases a cartridge with explosive. This cartridge, with a detonating cap on the bottom, drops upon a point and explodes the initial charge, which again explodes the charge in the mine.

In lifting the mine a rowboat with three men rows up over the mine, and by means of a tube shutting off the refraction of the light rays a person can look into the water. With a boat-hook and attached rope, a shackle on the top of the mine is caught, the pole unscrewed, the rope is taken into a winch aboard the steamer or barge, and the mine is then carefully hoisted. When the mine comes to the surface the mine engineer rows up, presses down a lever, and secures it with a steel pin. This performance locks the spring and prevents the cartridge from dropping on the piston. Next, the mine is hoisted on the barge, the top is unscrewed, and the cartridge holding the initial explosive charge is taken out, rendering the mine harmless with ordinary handling. The cylinder-like anchor is then hoisted by the attached cable, and last the weight is brought up.

We were busy hoisting and searching for mines till 3 p. m. Another tugboat, the *San Marco*, was also steaming around in our vicinity, keeping a sharp lookout for hostile men-of-war, and also, when seeing a mine, dropping a float. The fog had lifted a little, and once in a while we could see the outlines of houses on the shore. We had six mines on the barge and three on our steamer, when the launch which had taken me out hove in sight to take me back for dinner. Captain K—— said: "Well, we have been lucky so far; we have only one more mine to take up, and I had a good mind to blow it up and hike for home."

"Good," I said, "then I'll unpack my cameras again and take a picture of the explosion." At this moment the *San Marco* gave a signal of three short blasts. I looked toward the Italian coast and saw two men-of-war loom up in the fog; then two more. Two had four funnels each and were cruisers; the other two were torpedo-boat destroyers.

"Enemy in sight." "Clear the ship." "Jump aboard." "Cut the barge adrift," came in sharp commands from Captain K——.

Six men at the windlass were lowering a mine carefully onto the deck of the barge. They let it drop so suddenly that the men guiding it jumped aside in terror. All hands jumped from the barge aboard our steamer. The ropes holding the barge alongside were cut, the bells clanged in the engine-room, and we shot ahead. Fog had momentarily blotted the vessels out again and gave a false sense of security. "Make the towing hawser fast; we'll tow her," shouted K——. Three men tried to belay the hawser, but we had too much headway on already, and the rope tore through their fingers.

"Throw the bomb into her."

The bomb flew across, but fell short; then I saw a flash of lightning in the fog, and the next moment a huge fountain of water rose on our starboard side, and the shell flew screaming past us. Boom! boom! boom! Now all four ships gave us their broadsides and the stricken sea spouted geysers all around us and the *San Marco*. Screaming shells and roaring guns filled the fog.

"Twelve hundred meters," quoth K——. "They should soon get the range." I looked at our little Hotchkiss on the fore deck—there was no use to reply even. The *San Marco* had described a half-circle and came running up astern of us as if, like a good comrade, she was going to share our fate with us. As she came abreast of our Barge K—— shouted, "Drop a bomb into her."

"I have only one ready for my own ship," the captain yelled back.

"They will get our whole day's work," growled K——.

"Hurray!" we all shouted the next minute, as a shell struck the barge full center, exploding the six mines and shattering it in bits, enveloping all in a dense cloud of black smoke.

At this moment the other launch came alongside and raced along with us. I threw my cameras into it, and jumped aboard; then we sheared off again, so as not to give the enemy too big a target.

Next minute three shells shrieked so close to our ears that we threw ourselves flat in the bottom of the launch and one shaved the deck of No. 10. There seemed to be no escape. The Italians cut us off from Trieste, and we headed for Miramar. They did not come nearer; but the Lord knows they were near enough, and by rights they should have sent us to the bottom the first three shots. Even had they steamed directly up to us, they could have got us by the scruff of the neck in five minutes, for we could make only ten knots to their twenty-five.

One fast torpedo-boat, risking what was a few hours ago their own mine field, and, of course, knowing nothing to the contrary, got the No. 10 and our launch in line and gave us all attention in the manner of a pot-hunter trying to rake us. I had just taken my moving picture camera out of its case and set it on the tripod when a shell struck three feet from the launch, raising a big geyser. The column of water descending douched us and stopped our motor. I had to dry off the spark plugs while the engineer got busy cranking.

Happily, the motor sprang right on again, and I got back to the camera and commenced cranking. I tried to keep the No. 10 and the *San Marco* in the view-finder in case they should get hit, and endeavored to get the spouting of the shells. I got about one hundred feet of it, but it is a tame illustration of all the excitement of a race between life and death. The Italians with their speed, having passed us, now swung around again and edged us off from Miramar, so we held to the west of it for our shore batteries.

All this time we kept wondering why the next shell didn't strike one of us. Then we saw one of our submarines just diving to the periscope. By this time we came nearly within range of our shore batteries, and one of them began to bark at the Italians, but at such range and in the fog they must have just tried to scare them, for we couldn't even see the shells hitting the water. However, we escaped "by the skin of our teeth."

As the fog had lifted a little around noon, and we could see the houses on shore, evidently the lookouts had reported our presence and the Italians had left Grado to tackle us. The obscurity of the fog, the strange-looking barge, the *San Marco*, the proximity of the mine fields, all this had rendered the Italians so cautious that they were satisfied to run parallel with us and give us their broadside. The last we saw of them was when they swung more and more around toward their own coast and were again enveloped in the fog. They were the same four vessels that had bombarded us the day before, when I flew with Lieut. D—— in a hydroplane over Grado.

COSTS MORE NOW

Adam gave one rib and got a wife. Robert Kirton, of Pittsburgh, back from the front, lost seven ribs and then married his Red-Cross nurse. This shows the increased cost of living.

WEIGHTY MEASURES INVOLVING UNCLE SAM'S NAVY

THIS is the story of a conspiracy against Uncle Sam—a patriotic plot to be sure, for it is concerned with the son of a Spanish War veteran who was rejected for service in Uncle Sam's Navy because he was seven pounds shy of weight for height, the said son's up-and-down dimension being full six feet. It is a story of superfeeding conducted while the young man was skillfully kept a prisoner—albeit a willing one, but just to guard against his "jumping his feed"—by placing his nether garments carefully under lock and key. The New York *Sun* tells the tale and its happy outcome. It happened in this way:

Young Walter Francis everlastingly did want to get into the Navy and stop this *U*-boat nonsense once and for all. Wherefore last Saturday bright and early Potential Admiral Francis took his bearings from the compass he wears on his watch chain, yelled, "Ship ahoy!" to the skipper of a passing Brooklyn trolley car, boarded a starboard seat well aft in the car, and then set sail over the waves of Brooklyn asphalt toward the recruiting plant of the Second Naval Battalion of Brooklyn at the foot of Fifty-second street, Bay Ridge.

"Step on," directed the examining surgeon to young Mr. Francis, indicating the scales in his office. "Step off. Now step out—you're seven pounds shy for a six-footer."

Half an hour later Walter Francis, dejected and forlorn, appeared before his father.

"'Smatter, son?" inquired the Spanish War vet.

"'Smatter, pop! There's seven pounds the matter! Uncle Sam can do without me."

Mrs. Francis came into the room and heard the depressing news of her short-weight son, and straightway conspiracy stalked silently upon the scene. Says the writer in the *Sun:*

A moment later a significant look passed between father and mother above and back of the bowed head of their son. Mr. and Mrs. Francis withdrew to the kitchen for a council of war. Then Spanish-American War Veteran Joe Francis walked into the front room again and stood before his underweight offspring.

"Take off our pants, Walter," said Francis, senior, "And give me your—don't sit there staring at me; get busy—give me your shoes. Ma, catch the boy's pants when I throw 'em out to you. Lock his pants and shoes up with all his other pants and then start in cooking. Cook up everything you got in the house. And when you get a chance run down to Gilligan's and tell him to send up five pounds of dried apples."

"I'm on, pop!" suddenly shouted Embryo Admiral Walter Francis, springing to his feet alive once more. "You're going to feed me up for a couple of weeks so I'll make the weight. Gosh, you're there with the bean, pop—I never woulda thought of the scheme."

"For a couple of weeks!" cried Parent Francis scornfully. "For a couple of days, you mean, son. Come on into the dining-room and start right in to——. No, stay right where you are. Don't move from now on unless you have to or you might lose another ounce. You just sit right there all day. Ma will do the cooking and I'll be the waiter. And if you're not up to weight inside of three days then I'm a German spy. And don't weaken. Just keep in mind that even if you do it won't get you anything. For I'm going to keep the key to all your pants right in my pocket till you cripple the weighing scales. So all you're going to do from now on is stick around and eat."

Already Mrs. Francis had passed into the room a nightshirt and a three-quart pitcher brimming with sparkling Croton. Without a pause Parent Francis had filled a tumbler and passed it on to his offspring, who eagerly drained the glass. Tumbler after tumbler of water was tumbled into the digestive system of the underweight linotyper, while steadily from the kitchen came the happy sizzling of four pork chops and fast-frying potatoes with trimmings.

Twenty-one glasses of water disappeared into young Walter Francis before Saturday's sun had set, together with all the pork chops, the fried potatoes, thick slices of buttered bread, and some other snacks.

The Sunday treatment included fourteen glasses of water and a general packing-in of fattening fodder, until dinner-time arrived, when son Walter was fed up on two pounds of steak smothered in boiled potatoes with trimmings of stewed corn and mashed turnips, all resting on a solid foundation of well-buttered bread and roofed with a generous slab of apple pie. And then:

One and one-quarter pounds of mutton-chops merely formed the architectural approaches to the breakfast Walter Francis found staring him in the face when he arose heavily on Monday morning. Ham and eggs in groups—salty ham which hadn't been parboiled, thus retaining its thirst-arousing properties—was the centerpiece around which the luncheon Mrs. Francis had prepared that day for her son was draped. A dinner that ran all the way from soup to nuts (the time was growing short if Parent Francis was to make good on his promises) followed on Monday night, the big noise of the Monday dinner being a sirloin steak.

And just before Son Francis decided to call it a day and waddle to bed Spanish-American War Veteran Francis had a final happy thought. Father fed son a plentiful supply of dried apples and then unleashed a growler and went down to the corner and got a quart of collarless beer. Walter Francis flooded the dried apples with the entire quart of beer, cried "Woof! I'm a hippopotamus!" and collapsed into bed.

Tuesday morning last Father and Mother Francis personally helped their son toward the street-door after he had breakfasted on five pork-chops, two cups of coffee and four rolls. Once more he was about to set sail for the Second Naval Battalion recruiting office at the foot of Fifty-second Street, where three days earlier he had been turned down as hopelessly shy on tonnage. Parent Francis helped his bouncing boy aboard the trolley-car, shouting a last word of caution to walk, not run, to the nearest entrance to the recruiting station.

And just before young Mr. Francis applied again for the job of ridding the seas of *U*-boats (it should be mentioned incidentally that about half an hour earlier his father had unlocked a pair of pants and other gent's furnishings for the trip) the potential admiral saw the burnished sign on a corner saloon. He got off the car carefully, drank seven glasses of water in the saloon and then eased his way into the presence of the surgeon who had given him the gate on Saturday.

"I told you before you were many pounds underweight, young man," said the surgeon. "It's utterly useless for you to come around here when——"

"But that was away last week, Doc," wheezed young Mr. Francis. "Give me another try at your scales."

"My Gordon!" cried the surgeon, glancing at the scales and uttering his favorite cuss-word. "Saturday you were seven pounds under weight and to-day you're a pound overweight! How'd yuh ever do it?"

"I've heard of lads getting their teeth pulled to get out of serving Uncle Sam, but you're the first guy I ever heard of who made a fool of his stummick to get into the Navy," grinned Bos'n Carroll as Walter Francis bared his brawny arm for the vaccine. "Welcome to our ocean, Kid!"

NEVER TALK BACK

"——and then the Germans charged, and the captain shouted, 'Shoot at will,' and I shouted, 'Which one is he?' And then they took away my gun, and now I can't play any more."

GOING HOME

Visitor—"And what did you do when the shell struck you?"
Bored Tommy—"Sent mother a post-card to have my bed aired."

ENLISTED MEN TELL WHY THEY JOINED THE ARMY

OUR first forces in France were volunteers, part of the old regular Army, though many of the enlistments were recent. The motives leading men to join such an army are varied and in many cases humorous or pathetic. A Y. M. C. A. secretary in France, who had won the confidence of the men with whom he was associated, wondered why each man had come. So he arranged that they should hand in cards telling why they had enlisted. Mr. Arthur Gleason presents some of the answers in the New York *Tribune* as "the first real word from the soldier himself of why he has offered himself." These replies came from two battalions of an infantry regiment, which, for military reasons can not be identified. Mr. Gleason puts them in several groups. One is the sturdily patriotic. Thus, one soldier says:

"My reason in 1907 was that I liked the service and wanted to try for something new and bright for my country."

Others say: "Because my country needs me"; "to catch Villa"; "I wanted to get the Kaiser's goat"; "for the benefit of the American Army"; "so patriotic and didn't know what it was"; "Mexican trouble, 1917"; "I felt like my country needed me, and I wanted to do something for it, and that was the only way I was able to do anything for my dear country, the good old U. S. A."; "I never did anything worth while on the outside, so I dedicated myself to my country that I might be of some use to some one"; "a couple of Germans"; "to serve God and my country."

Another class of answers deal with what is in the blood of youth—the desire to taste adventure, to see the world, and see France. Here are a few in this group:

"To do my duty and see the world"; "to see the world, ha! ha!"; "because I thought I would like that kind of a life, and didn't know what kind of a life I would have to lead in this hole"; "got tired of staying at home"; "I was seeking adventure and change of environments"; "to kill time and fight"; "to see France"; "I was discouraged with the civilian life and wanted to get some excitement"; "to have a chance to ride on the train; I never had ridden"; "they said I was not game and I was, and because I wished to"; "because I wouldn't stay in one place any length of time, I thought if I joined the Army for three or seven years I would be ready to settle down. I think that is as good a thing as any boy could do"; "to see the world"; "I had tried everything else, so I thought I would try the Army."

Another group of answers deal with the individual human problem of hunger and loneliness. These that follow illustrate this:

"To fight, and for what money was in it"; "three good square meals and a bath"; "because I was disgusted with myself and thought it would make a man out of me"; "I was too lazy to do anything else"; "I was stewed"; "to get some clothes, a place to sleep and something to eat"; "because I was hungry"; "because I was nuts with the dobey heat" (dobey is a Mexican slang word brought up by the boys from the border); "because I had to keep from starving;" "in view of the fact that I was so delicate and a physical wreck I joined the Army, hoping to get lots of fresh air and exercise, which I have sure gotton, and am ready to go home at any time"; "I was in jail and they came and got me. Hard luck!"; "because I did not have no home"; "I got hungry"; "pork and beans were high at the time"; "three square meals a day and a flop."

The voice of State rights speaks in the replies of two men from the South:

"To represent the State of Kentucky."

"In answer to a call from my State, Mississippi, and to see something of the world, and I have seen some of the world, too."

Then, too, there are a number that refuse to be classified; each has its own note of suffering or audacity of humor:

"To catch the Kaiser"; "because the girls like a soldier"; "because my girl turned her back on me, that's all"; "I thought I was striking something soft, but ..."; "the dear ones at home"; "I was crazy"; "two reasons: because girls like soldiers and I saw a sign '500,000 men wanted to police up France'"; "for my health and anything else that is in it" (a consumptive soldier); "to show that my blood was made of the American's blood"; "to learn self-control"; "it was a mistake; I didn't know any better"; "for my adopted country"; "I got drunk on Saturday, the Fourth of July, 1913, and I left home on the freight-train and joined the Army, and woke up the next morning getting two sheets in the wind, and I haven't got drunk since that; made a man out of me"; "to keep from working, but I got balled"; "I have not seen anything yet but rain"; "because I didn't know what I was doing"; "to kill a couple of Germans for the wrong done Poland"; "to keep from wearing my knuckles out on the neighbors' back doors"; "adventure and experience; also, to do my little bit for my country, the good old U. S. A., and the Stars and Stripes, the flag of freedom"; "to fight for my country and the flag, for the U. S. is a free land, and we will get the Kaiser, damn him. Oh, the U. S. A.!" (Picture of a flag.)

One man makes out a complete category of his reasons: (*a*) "To see excitement"; (*b*) "to help win this war and end the Kaiser's idea of world ruler"; (*c*) "help free the German people from Kaiserism."

And, finally, there is one that needs no comment, and with this we will end: "Because mother was dead and I had no home."

THE NATIONAL GAME

Teacher—"What lessons do we learn from the attack on the Dardanelles?"
Prize Scholar—"That a strait beats three kings, dad says."

TOMMY ATKINS, RAIN-SOAKED AND WAR-WORN STILL GRINS

FREDERIC WILLIAM WILE, one of the Vigilantes, differs with Sherman in declaring that war is mud. He had just returned from what he describes as one of the periodical joy-rides which the British Foreign Office and the General Staff organize from time to time to give civilians an opportunity to visit the front. Mr. Wile's visits occurred when the war-god was evidently taking a much-needed rest, for he says that on two occasions when he intruded upon Armageddon he saw more rain than blood spilled. But he found Tommy Atkins—mud-caked and rain-soaked—still wearing the grin that won't come off. Mr. Wile thus writes of his last visit:

I am in to-night from a day in the trenches. It rained all the time. The trenches were gluey and sticky, and the "duck-boards" along which we traveled were afloat a good share of the day. But the only people who used really strong language about having to eat, sleep, and navigate in such soggy territory was our party of civilian tenderfoots. The cave-dwellers in khaki whom we encountered in endless numbers were as happy as school-children on a picnic. Clay-spattered from head to foot, their clothes often wringing wet, they looked up from whatever happened to be their tasks and grinned as we passed.

Our chief and always dominating impression was of their grins and smiles. I am firmly convinced that soldiers who can laugh in such weather can not be overcome by anything, not even the Prussian military machine. Perhaps Tommy smiled more broadly than usual to-day at our expense, for during our hike from a certain quarry to a certain front line "Fritz" sent over whiz-bangs which caused us arm-chair warriors from home to duck and dodge in the most un-Napoleonic fashion, even though our gyrations were in obedience to nature's first law—self-preservation.

When you're in a trench and a shell screeches through the heavens—you always hear it and never see it—the temptation to side-step is the last word in irresistibility. You have been provided with a steel helmet before starting out on the expedition in view of the possibility that a stray piece of German shrapnel may come your way. These helmets have saved many a gallant Tommy from sudden death.

After you've heard a whiz-bang and find that you are still intact, you ask: "Was that a *Boche* or one of ours?" You experience an indefinable sense of relief when you are told that it was "one of ours," but you keep on ducking in the same old way whenever the air is rent.

Yes, it is the invincible grin of Tommy Atkins in abominable atmospheric surroundings and in the omnipresent shadow of death that has photographed itself most indelibly on my memory to-day. But next to that I am struck by his amazing good health as mirrored by his ruddy cheeks and bright eyes. Certainly the strapping young fellows whom I have seen are a vastly finer, sturdier lot, physically viewed, than any set of men now running around the streets of London in citizens' clothes. It is manifestly "the life," this endless sojourn of theirs on the edge of No Man's Land, with the enemy a rifle-shot away.

You ask their officers what explains this hygienic phenomenon—this ability to keep at the top note of "fitness" amid privations almost unimaginable. You will be told that it is the remorselessly "regular life" the men lead for one thing, and the liberal supply of fresh air, for another. Then it is the simple food they eat and the never-ending exercise they get for their legs and arms and muscles. They sleep when and where they can, in their clothes for weeks on end, never saying "How-do-you-do?" to a bath-tub sometimes for many days, though they shave each morning with religious punctuality, even in the midst of a mighty "push." Cleanliness of physiognomy is as much a passion with Mr. Atkins as his daily ablutions are to a pious Turk. You will go far before you will find a cleaner-faced aggregation of young men than the British Army in the field.

Should you have any doubt as to what the physical appearance of the men tells you, and ask an officer how Tommy is standing the strain of the war, he declares enthusiastically, "The men are simply splendid!" And you hear from the men that the officers are "top-hole." But all that you will learn from the officers on that subject is:

Regulation No. 1, when a man gets a commission in the British Army, is: "Men first, officers next." An officer's business, in other words, is to see that his men are well looked after. If there is any time left when he has done that, he may look after himself. But Tommy comes first. That is why the relations between superior and subordinate in the mighty Citizens' Army of Britain are perfect in the highest degree. Duke's son and cook's son are real pals. Class distinctions are non-existent in the England that is the trenched fields of France and Flanders.

"Just so we keep on livin'—that's all we ask," was the sententious observations of a mud-clotted Yorkshireman who backed against the slimy wall of a trench to let us pass. We had asked him the stereotyped question—"Well, Tommy, how goes it?" His answer was unmistakably typical of the spirit which dominates the whole army. The men are not happy to be there. They long for the war to end. They do not put in their time in the slush and rain cheering and singing. They hanker for "Blighty." They want to go home. But not until the grim business that brought them to France is satisfactorily finished. They want no Stockholm-made peace. They are fighting for a knock-out.

I left behind me in London a lot of dismal, gloomy, and down-hearted friends, candidates all for the Pessimists' Club. I wish they could have hiked through the trenches with me. It is the finest cure in the world for the blues. It may thunder and pour day and night in Trenchland, and the country may be a morass for miles in every direction, but the sun of optimism and confidence is always shining in the British Army's heart.

SOMETHING NEW FOR THE MARINES

"IF CORPORAL —— ever wrote a better story for his newspaper than the one he has sent to us, I should certainly like to read it." This high praise comes from Maj. W. H. Parker, head of the Marine Recruiting Service in New York, and is bestowed upon a letter in *The Recruiters' Bulletin*, which was written by a marine, formerly a reporter in Philadelphia and now "Somewhere in France." He rejoices at the start that "at last it is happening," which "happening" is that the marines, "every scrapping one of them down to the last grizzled veteran, are undergoing new experiences—learning new tricks." Of course this is beyond possibility, everybody will say, and the ex-reporter admits that—

One would think so after hearing of their experiences in far-away China, Japan, and the Philippines, near-by Cuba, Haiti, and Mexico, and other places which God forgot and which you and I never heard of; after hearing stories of daredevil bravery, fierce abandon and disregard for life and limb in the faithful discharge of their duties as soldiers of the sea and guardians of the peace in Uncle Sam's dirty corners.

And yet here in France, among people of their own color and race, of paved streets and taxicabs, among the old men and women of the villages, among the *poilus* coming and going in a steady stream to and from the front, the marine is learning new things every day.

Packing up "back home" on a few hours' notice is no new experience to the marine. Marching aboard a transport, with the date and hour of sailing unknown, is taken as a matter of course by the veteran. There is no cheering gallery, no weeping relatives, wife, or sweethearts, as he leaves to carry out the business in hand. It is just the same as if you were going to your office in the morning. You may return in time for dinner or you may be delayed. The only difference is that sometimes the marines do not return.

Although life aboard the transport which carried the first regiment of marines to new fields of action in France was a matter of routine to the average sea-going soldier, there was added the zest of expectation of an encounter with one of the floating perils, the "sub." It was but a matter of two or three days, however, when everyone became accustomed to the numerous lookouts stationed about the ship, the frequent "abandon ship" drills, the strange orders which came down the line, and the new-fangled rules and regulations which permitted no lights or smoking after sundown.

Kaiser "Bill's" pet sharks were contemptuously referred to as the "tin lizzies" of the sea. "We must play safe and avoid them," was the policy of those entrusted with the safety of more than 2,000 expectant fighters, however. And we met them, too. Not one or two of them, but—(here the censor interfered.)

Since his arrival in France the marine has spent day after day in learning new things, not the least of which is that contrary to his usual experience of finding about him a hostile people, rifle in hand, and unknown danger ahead, he is among a people who welcome him as a friend and ally in the struggle against a common enemy. With the arrival of the American troops, the appealing outstretched hands of France were changed to hands of welcome, creating an atmosphere that might easily have turned the heads of men more balanced than the marines after being confined for more than two weeks aboard a ship, but—

Here, again, one comes in contact with the matter-of-fact administration of the marines. Arriving under such circumstances, the landing and encampment of the marines were effected with a military precision and businesslike efficiency which allowed no one for a moment to forget the serious nature of the mission upon which he had embarked.

Stores and supplies were loaded on trucks and, in less than three hours after the order was given to disembark, the marines, with their packs strapped over the shoulders, were marching to their camp just on the outskirts of the seaport town of ———. Within another hour the whole regiment was under canvas, field-desks and typewriter-chests were unlocked, and regimental and other department offices were running along at full swing.

And that was the beginning of the period of training during which the marine is learning everything that is to be known about waging twentieth-century warfare. He is taking a post-graduate course in the intricacies of modern trench-building, grenade-throwing, and barbed-wire entanglements. And the very best men of the French Army are his instructors.

The marine is also learning the "lingo" of this country, the nicer phrases of the language as well as the slang of the trenches. But in the majority of cases experience was his teacher. Upon the arrival of the transport liberty hours were arranged for the marines, and, armed with a "Short Vocabulary of French Words and Phrases," with which all had been supplied, they invaded the cafés, restaurants, and shops of the little old seaport town.

And it was the restaurants where one's ignorance of French was most keenly felt. All sorts of queer and yet strangely familiar noises emanated from the curtained windows of the *buvettes* along the streets. Upon investigation it would be discovered that a marine, having lost his "vocabulary," was flapping his arms and cackling for eggs, earnestly baahing for a lamb stew, or grunting to the best of his ability in a vain endeavor to make *madame* understand that he wanted roast pork. Imagine his chagrin to find that "pig" and "pork," as shown on page 16, are "*porc*" in French and are pronounced just the same as in good old American. But the scenes that presented themselves on Sundays or *fête* days—take the 4th or 14th of July, for example—were such as never had been seen in any French town before. Picture a tiny café, low and whitewashed, ancient, weather-beaten, but immaculately clean, with its heavy ceiling-beams and huge fireplace with brass and copper furnishings. With this background imagine just as many tables as the little place can hold about which are crowded French and American soldiers, sailors, and marines.

The table in the corner there, for instance: two *poilus*, two American "jackies," two marines, and an old Breton peasant farmer with his wife, fat, uncomprehending, and wild-eyed, and his daughter, red-lipped and of fair complexion—these three in from the country for a holiday, the women arrayed in the black cloth and velvet costumes, bright-colored silk aprons, and elaborate linen head-dress which identify them as native of a certain locality.

One of the "jackies" sings with gusto service songs of strong and colorful language, singing to himself save for the half-amused and wondering stares of the peasants. The younger of the Frenchmen shows by taking off his coat and unbuttoning his shirt where the shell-fragment penetrated which caused the paralysis in his left arm and sent him home on a month's furlough, and the Americans eye with interest the actual fragment itself, now doing duty as a watch-charm.

But the hubbub and racket cease, and every one rushes to the windows and door as the Marine Band comes swinging along the water-front, playing with catching rhythm "Our

Director." The French burst out in cries of "*Vive l'Amérique!*" The fever spreads, and our soldiers and sailors yell "*Vive la France!*" or as near to it as they can get, as the procession marches by, and the fat old peasant woman says with full approval, "That's beautiful!"

Another letter from the permanent training-camp of the marines, published in *The Recruiters' Bulletin*, tells of an inspection of the regiment by General Pershing and General Pétain, the French Commander-in-Chief. We read "that the piercing eyes of 'Black Jack' rarely miss an unshaven face, badly polished shoes, or the sloppy appearance of anyone" among the soldiers under inspection, and the writer relates:

Together with the Commander-in-Chief of all the French forces and accompanied by several French generals, representing the most important military units in France, General Pershing made one of his now famous whirlwind inspection tours and descended upon the marines amid a cloud of dust which marked the line of travel of the high-powered French touring-cars which carried the generals. Not so very long before that the field-telephone in the regimental office rang and a voice came over the wire:

"The big blue machine is on the way down, and will probably be there in ten minutes." That was sufficient. Two or three telephone-calls were hurriedly made, and the Colonel, accompanied by his staff, proceeded on "up the line," met the General's party, and the marines were ready.

The result of the inspection is summed up in the memorandum issued to the command and which says in part: "Yesterday, at the inspection of the regiment by General ——, Commander-in-Chief of all the French forces, General Pershing, Commander-in-Chief of the American forces in France, and General ——, commanding the —— Division Chasseurs, who are instructing our men, General —— congratulated the Colonel of our regiment on the splendid appearance of officers and men as well as the cleanliness of the town. General Pershing personally told the regimental commander that he wished to congratulate him on having such an excellent regiment."

This announcement was read to the marines as they were lined up for their noonday meal. And where is the marine whose chest would not swell just a bit at this tribute paid by General Pershing to those upon whose shoulders rests the responsibility of maintaining and perpetuating the glorious history and fine traditions of the United States Marine Corps?

JUDGING BY HIS LETTERS

"Where's your uncle, Tommy?"

"In France."

"What is he doing?"

"I think he has charge of the war."

BLESS THESE AMATEURS

"What are you knitting, my pretty maid?"

She purled, then dropped a stitch.

"A sock or a sweater, sir," she said,

"And darned if I know which!"

NEW GROUNDS FOR EXEMPTION

The two young girls watched the "nutty young Cuthbert" pass along the street.

"Did he appeal for exemption?" said May.

"Yes," said Ray, "you might have known he would."

"On what grounds?"

"I don't know," replied Ray, "unless it was upon the ground that if he went to the war his wife's father would have no son-in-law to support."

SOUSA'S LITTLE JOKE

Lieut. John Philip Sousa, who is organizing military bands for the navy, was talking to a correspondent about the submarine danger.

"A friend of mine, a cornet virtuoso," he said, "was submarined in the Mediterranean. The English paper that reported the affair worded it thus:

"'The famous cornetist, Mr. Hornblower, though submarined by the Germans in the Mediterranean, was able to appear at Marseilles the following evening in four pieces.'"

RAPID MILITARY ADVANCEMENT

A certain west end tailor, being owed a considerable amount by a colonel who was received everywhere in society, made a bargain with the gentleman. He stipulated that instead of paying his debt, the colonel should introduce himself and family into high society. To this the colonel agreed and not long after the tailor received an invitation to dinner.

When the tailor arrived in the full glory of a perfect evening dress, the colonel did not recognize him.

"Pardon me, my dear fellow," he said quietly, as he shook hands, "I quite forget your name!"

"Quite likely!" sneered the tailor, also sotto voce. "But I made your breeches!"

"Ah, yes!" said the colonel, smiling. And then, turning to his wife, said: "Allow me to introduce you, dear—Major Bridges!"

Printed in Great Britain
by Amazon